Brett Wilson and de Soto's Cross

John V. Suter

CrossLink Publishing
RAPID CITY, SD

Suter/CrossLink Publishing
1601 Mt. Rushmore Rd. Ste 3288
Rapid City, SD 57701
www.CrossLinkPublishing.com

Ordering Information:
Quantity sales. Special discounts are available on quantity purchases by corporations, associations, and others. For details, contact the "Special Sales Department" at the address above.

Brett Wilson and de Soto's Cross/John V. Suter.
—1st ed.

ISBN 978-1-63357-244-7

Library of Congress Control Number: 2021946426

To Rebecca, Rory, and Garrett.
Every adventure is extraordinary

Contents

The Incomplete Memory

It is another warm morning in Camden, Tennessee. The sun is just now rising over the tall, long-needle pines that line the perimeter of the pasture on Grandpa Jake's farm. The goats leap and run playfully in the fresh morning air as the sun paints the greens and grays of the trees with bright splotches of gold and orange. Brett is sitting with her back resting against a mound of hay as she chews on a stalk of brittle yellow grass.

She stares up at the brilliant sunrise. Her Royals hat is pulled down over her eyes, shielding them from the vibrant yellow light. She chews more forcefully on the hay stem, absently moving it from one side of her mouth to the other.

Brett closes her eyes. She can feel the sun on her eyelids, the heat taking her back to the deep canyons of New Mexico. Two weeks ago, she was staring into the ancient city of Cibola, a city that hadn't been seen in a few hundred years. It had been within her reach. She had located the place where her dad had gone, and as quickly as it appeared in the rocky canyon, the shining city vanished. Her father is lost somewhere out there and it is up to her to find him. The weight of the task presses on her shoulder. It feels like it will push her flat on the ground. . .

She spits the folded wet stem of grass out of her mouth and gets quickly to her feet. She brushes away the grass clinging to her cargo pants, and the brittle stems flutter to the ground.

She reaches down and picks up a tattered brown book sitting beside the mound of hay. She holds the book tightly in her hands and walks slowly out toward the frolicking goats. She had used the book to locate Cibola. It had been her guide on the journey into the past as she explored the tale of Esteban and Coronado. It had led her to the door that opened into the marvelous golden city. It had been her dad's field book . . . but here she is now, walking through the tall yellow stalks of grass. on her grandpa's farm in Camden, Tennessee.

Brett places the weathered book into a side pocket of her pants and shoves her hands deep into her pockets. She walks through the swaying orchard grass as she nears Kitty and Julie, two of her favorite Lamancha goats. Each goat in the herd bounds in her direction as she draws near. Kitty, the black goat, kicks her legs wildly behind her as she dances toward her. Brett holds out her hand and pats the side of Kitty's face. "Having fun?" Kitty tilts her head, enjoying the attention. "You like this better, don't you?" Julie steps up to Brett's other side, waiting her turn. "Okay." Brett begins rubbing Julie in the same place. "Don't want to be left out, do you?"

"Nobody ever wants to be left out," says a friendly voice.

Brett turns. Behind her stands Natalie, a broad smile spread across her face. "Right on time, boss," Natalie says. Brett pats the goats on their heads and walks toward Natalie.

"Ready to talk to Dr. Mies?"

Natalie nods her head slowly. "Let's do it."

They start across the field toward the distant barn. As they walk in silence, Natalie casts side-long glances at Brett. Brett looks at her friend questioningly. "What?"

"I snuck right up behind you, and you had no idea I was there," Natalie says slowly.

"That's what you've been trying to say to me for the last five minutes?"

"You had no idea." A smile spreads across her face. "That is totally awesome."

"Yeah. Yeah." Brett smiles.

"All these abilities I never knew I had are now getting stronger and stronger."

"Abilities?" Brett asks in surprise.

"Yeah. Taking that bad guy out with my softball skills." Natalie swings wildly with an imaginary bat. "Fighting those guys in the canyon." She continues kicking and punching in all directions. "Stealthily walking across a field without making a sound," she says, looking left and right and silently placing her feet softly on the ground. "I mean *wow*. Abilities."

"I see," Brett laughs.

"You're safe with me around, Brett."

"I'm sure of that more than your abilities."

"What?"

"I heard you coming."

"Now you're just being mean."

Brett laughs as they near the barn, her laughter echoing off the two-story metal siding. It is the first time she has truly laughed in the last two weeks. All of her attention has been focused on formulating a plan for getting back into Cibola, so she hasn't spent much time with Natalie—or with anyone else for that matter. She has been counting down the minutes until she could speak with Dr. Mies.

Dr. Mies has been in the hospital for the last two weeks. For some reason, his recovery slowed. The doctors tried everything to help but his body just didn't respond. But over the last two days, Dr. Mies has improved so much that they finally let him go home. Brett has to see him. She has to know what he meant when he said, "Esteban is the key. Rock needs Esteban." Brett is going to get the answers to her questions and use her dad's journal to find Cibola again. This time she is bringing him home.

Brett opens the door to the barn and pulls her bike out from the hay covered stall. Natalie's bike is leaning against the side of the barn as they continue toward the gate. The wheels squeak loudly. "You might need to oil that." Natalie says holding her ears. "Maybe later." Brett responds dryly. Natalie smiles. "Right. It is time to interrogate Dr. Mies. No time for jokes."

Natalie grabs the handlebars of her bike and pushes it along beside Brett. They walk in silence through the metal gate that swings freely on its hinge. After Brett and Natalie pass through, Brett latches the gate. She turns quickly and hops on her bike. "We can still have some fun before we get there." She laughs as she pedals away from Natalie toward the main road. "Not fair." Natalie yells behind her. They race along the curvy streets for five minutes getting closer and closer to the middle of Camden. The wind blows through the blonde hair that sticks out from under her baseball cap as Brett rides her bike through the residential district of downtown Camden. She races by the two-story Victorian homes that line the street. She steers sharply onto the sidewalk pedaling faster and faster. She looks behind her as Natalie veers onto the sidewalk and yells, "This is great!"

Brett laughs as she turns onto North Street. She peddles faster toward a tall polished white house at the end of the street. Ordinarily Dr. Mies has a well-kept house with flawless paint and bright clear windows. The house is still immaculate, but the grass and other plants in the yard have become grossly overgrown. Brett turns onto the driveway and rolls to a stop at the front step. Natalie screeches to a halt beside her. Brett looks over at her slowly. "Sorry," Natalie says. "That was a little too loud." Natalie jumps off her bike and steps into the tall, brown grass. "You know, he could use a lawnmower guy."

"I doubt he's even thought about it."

"Right. Right. Lost in a disappearing city and then in the hospital."

"Might make you forget. Let's just hope he remembers how he got out of the city—and what my dad needs."

Brett swings her leg over the bike and walks up the whitewashed wooden steps. Her face is hard as she takes the five steps up to the dark brown door. Her heart starts beating faster and faster with each slow step. Her breath catches in her chest. She stands motionless, staring at the golden knocker. Her mind wanders to the questions she has ready to ask. The questions that will start the process of locating her dad.

Natalie steps up beside her, first staring at the door and then looking at Brett. "Are we going to knock or are we going to stand a little longer?" Brett glances over at her and Natalie smiles broadly. "Trying to relieve some of the tension." Brett raises her hand slowly and taps the knocker lightly against the door. The slight *tap, tap, tap* resonates through the door into her fingers. She takes her hand away and waits. The seconds drag on for what seems like forever. Brett shifts her weight from her left to her right foot, trying to do something to pass the time.

"I don't think he heard you knocking," Natalie whispers.

"Why are you whispering?"

"I'm not sure," Natalie says, still whispering. "Maybe you should knock again."

"Maybe you're right," Brett whispers. "Now you have me doing it."

As Brett reaches again for the knocker, the door handle starts to turn. "He's here," Natalie says in a very faint voice. The door opens slowly, revealing Dr. Mies standing in the doorway, grimacing. His face is sunken, his shoulders slumped forward. He looks like he is ready to collapse.

"I wondered when you would come and see me," he says hoarsely. "Come in." He turns and hobbles down the narrow hallway. Brett and Natalie exchange concerned looks and quickly follow.

Natalie closes the door. They stand watching Dr. Mies as he gingerly places one foot in front of the other. "I'm better," he says without turning around. "You don't need to fear for my condition." He grabs the doorframe at the end of the hall to hold himself up and turns, a small smile spreading across his face. Brett's presses her lips tightly together and her eyes narrow slightly as she rubs the tip of her chin. "Rock has the same expression," he says. Hearing her dad's name sends a cold, pulsating tremor through Brett's body.

"Right," she says, forcing a smile.

Dr. Mies turns and walks slowly into the paneled living room and falls into a dark brown recliner, motioning Brett toward the worn leather sofa. He leans back into the folds of the recliner and closes his eyes. His breathing is heavy and labored, and Brett can hear a faint wheeze escape every time he exhales. She takes a seat on the edge of the couch and looks up as Natalie enters the room.

Dr. Mies slowly opens his eyes. "Take a seat," he says. Natalie hesitates, then walks across the room and sits next to Brett. Natalie grabs Brett's arm as she stares at Dr. Mies. "What are you doing?" Brett says softly. "Sorry." Natalie scoots a few inches away. Brett turns and smiles at Dr. Mies. "Sorry to bother you, Dr. Mies," Brett starts. She looks over at Natalie. Dr. Mies coughs loudly, pulls a handkerchief from his pocket, and wipes away the saliva from his lips.

"Excuse me," he says, before a series of violent coughs shake his whole body.

Brett and Natalie exchange worried looks. "We can come back later," Brett says in a soothing voice.

Dr. Mies holds up his hand as he wipes more of the thick saliva away. "No. I am ready to help you."

Brett takes a deep breath as she prepares to pepper Dr. Mies with the questions she has rehearsed hundreds of times in her mind. Like a lawyer examining a witness, she has her questions framed in a way to get the appropriate response. What did he mean when he said, "Esteban is the key. Rock needs Esteban"?

She had thought about that for two weeks straight, and it always left her head hurting. Why would her dad need Esteban? Wasn't he in the city with Esteban? She had looked tirelessly through the worn brown book, and nothing in it offered an adequate explanation. Now here she is, looking at Dr. Mies sympathetically, ready to barrage him with question after question.

"Dr. Mies. Why does my dad need Esteban?"

"I'm sorry?" he asks with his brow furrowed.

"The day you came out of the city, you said that Rock needs Esteban."

"I said that?" His eyes get wider.

"Yes, you did," Brett replies softly, as if talking to a young child.

Dr. Mies closes his eyes and settles down deeper into the chair. His pale hand slowly moves upward and begins rubbing the side of his head. "Dr. Mies," Brett continues, "don't you remember?" Tears leak out of his tightly closed eyes as he rubs his face more vigorously. Brett glances at Natalie, who stares back at her with wide eyes. "What did you mean? Please tell me. I need this information if I'm going to find dad."

Brett sits up on the edge of the couch as she waits for a response. She stares intently at his frail, withered face. His hand falls onto his lap and his shoulders slump forward. It looks like he is ready to fall out of his chair. Brett exchanges a worried look with Natalie, who shrugs her shoulders. Brett's gaze returns to the fragile Dr. Mies. His eyes open quickly and begin to dart around the room. Fear spreads across his pale face as he catches sight of Brett watching him. His hands start shaking violently and his feet tap vigorously against the wooden floor.

"Dr. Mies!" Brett cries, not knowing what else to say.

"You are safe at home," Natalie interjects.

Dr. Mies slides down further in the chair as the motion in his body presses him closer to the floor. This is how he was acting when they found him in the canyon. When he uttered the words "Rock needs Esteban." Brett stands up and slowly walks over to his shaking form. She glances back at Natalie. Natalie shakes her head, but Brett kneels beside the chair. She extends her hand toward the doctor's shaking body. Brett is sure this is the right thing to do. She is sure that Dr. Mies will tell her the information she needs.

She places her hand on his arms and speaks in a delicate, soothing voice, "Dr. Mies, Rock needs your help." The confidence builds inside her as more words materialize in her head. "You need to remember Cibola. You need to remember why Rock needs Esteban." She is speaking in a melodious voice, like a hypnotist. She doesn't believe in hypnosis, but whatever works to help Dr. Mies release his memories, she will do.

His eyes flutter and slowly close. The terror displayed on his face softens and his breathing becomes steady and light. He stops shaking as Brett continues. "Can you recall what it is like in Cibola?" She waits silently as she watches the lines on his face relax. He looks like he is in a deep sleep. His eyes open slowly, and he stares at her.

"It is so beautiful that words cannot describe the grandeur of it. The golden walls shimmering in the bright afternoon sun. The golden streets meandering through the central portion of the city. It takes my breath away." A smile spreads across his face.

"What else do you remember?"

"The stillness of the air is soothing, and the silence allowed you to hear the faintest sounds transmitted through the city. It gives you a sense of peace that nothing on earth could ever give."

"How did you get there?"

"A doorway. A doorway lit by the most vibrant light that I have ever seen. Like being right next to the sun. We just walked into it, and there we were with all the others."

Brett glances at Natalie. The realization that there are others in the city causes the hair to stand up on her arms. She wants to ask a question about the people, but she decides against it. She must keep her query focused on how to locate her dad. She looks back at Dr. Mies. His face is relaxed, and he smiles at her.

"What did you do while you were there?" Brett says softly.

"We explored. Rock wanted to know every-thing. He asked the people questions about how they came to live in the city. Where they came from. How old they were. Unfortunately for him, he didn't have his field book. He could have filled up every page with the number of questions he asked."

Brett reaches down and feels the book inside her pocket. She wishes he had it now instead of her. "Did you find Esteban?" The smile on his face quickly fades. He begins rubbing his face.

"I don't remember," he says, his voice trailing off. Brett looks at him intently, trying to will his memory to release the information.

"How did you get out?" She holds her breath, waiting for him to respond. His eyes flutter and she can feel tremors starting to pulse in his shoulders. She lets out a ragged breath. "Dr. Mies, can you tell me?" She grips his shoulder tightly.

"I'm sorry," he says slowly, "I have no idea how I got out of there. I can see the city. The people that we met. What they were wearing. The smells and sounds, but for some reason how I made my way out, I can't recall."

Brett pats his shoulder lightly, trying to calm the tremors that are building in magnitude. "Don't worry, Dr. Mies," she says. "You have helped us."

"You are being kind," he says, "Unfortunately the memories that will help you are locked away somewhere up here." He continues pointing at his head.

"We will find him." Brett says confidently.

Dr. Mies looks away. Brett still has her hand on his shoulder. The vibrations moving through his body begin to slow once again and he starts to regain his normal state. Brett stands up. "Thank you for all the information."

Dr. Mies reaches up and places his pale white hand on hers. "I wish I could do more." Brett nods and motions to Natalie that it's time to leave. Natalie stands and walks toward the doorway. Brett squeezes the doctor's hand and turns to leave, then stops. "I have one more question, Dr. Mies."

"Ask away."

"Was Esteban there?"

"From what the people said, he has moved on to another city."

"Really."

"That is what they believed."

"So, there are more than one?"

"They said there are seven to be exact, but I'm not sure what to make of that."

"That is interesting."

"Don't know if it is probable."

Brett stands with her back to him as she begins processing this new information. The people claim there are other cities like Cibola. If that is the case, how would she go about looking for them? Esteban is now in one of these other cities. If her dad needs Esteban, she needs to locate him.

She walks slowly toward the door. A final question materializes in her head. "How long were you there?" She waits at the doorway for a response.

"A week I would guess." Brett looks up at the ceiling, taking in the answer.

"Thank you, Dr. Mies," she says as she exits the room.

CHAPTER 2

Dead End

Brett walks out the door and holds onto the handle, making sure it closes softly. She lets the door latch securely, then thrusts her hands deep inside her pants pockets. She stares intently down at the wooden floorboards as she absentmindedly begins walking toward the steps. Her mind focuses on the words Dr. Mies just spoke to her. "Esteban is in another city." Her thoughts dart from the image of Cibola and the delight of finding it to the daunting reality that there are other cities—six, if Dr. Mies is correct. The force of that reality presses on her like a fist against bread dough. The pressure threatens to compress her brain into the tiniest of particles.

Brett looks up as she comes to the wooden steps. Natalie is leaning against the railing, staring at Brett with her brow furrowed as if to ask, "What just happened in there?"

Brett shrugs. "Not sure what to make of it." Her mind is still thinking about the other cities, about how to find Esteban, and about how that can lead her to her dad.

A thought rushes into her mind like a flooded river after a storm. Maybe her dad has moved to another city. How will she find him if that is the case? She steps awkwardly on the step and her foot slips downward. She feels pressure on her right arm and looks over quickly. Natalie is holding the upper part of her arm so tightly that her fingers are turning a dull red color. "That was close." Natalie says slowly.

"I guess I should watch where I am going," she says with a smile.

"Maybe."

Brett walks down the steps cautiously while Natalie follows closely behind her. Once at the bottom, Brett's mind moves again to the questions she needs answered. She is walking quickly; she can hear Natalie panting behind her, trying to keep up. "How am I going to find Esteban?" she mutters. "Where are the other cities? Can you find them using electromagnetics?"

Natalie runs up beside her. "Not sure what you're saying," she says. Brett glances at her. Her eyes are bright and dancing in their sockets.

"He said there were other cities, and Esteban is in one of them."

Natalie stops abruptly, her mouth sagging open. "What? How?"

"Not sure."

"He could be messed up. He was acting all weird the day we found him. Maybe the city did something to his mind," Natalie says with her tongue hanging out and her eyes crossing as she staggers around in a circle.

"Could be, but we need to check."

They reach their bicycles. Natalie flings her leg over the frame and settles onto the seat. "You think there are others, don't you?" Brett climbs onto her bike and looks at her with narrowed eyes.

"The legend says that there are seven cities of gold." Brett sets her right foot on the pedal and presses down hard. The bike moves quickly away from Natalie. "I need to talk to your mom!" she yells as she speeds down the tree-lined road.

The wind whips at Brett's face as she speeds away from Dr. Mies's house and through the vacant streets toward Camden College. She looks back; Natalie is twenty feet behind her, pedaling faster and faster trying to catch up. "If you want to talk to my mom, you better wait for me!" she yells. Brett slows her pedaling as Natalie races up beside her, breathing heavily. "Thanks for waiting," she says through quick breaths.

Brett laughs. "I need you to talk to your mom."

"She likes you better than me anyway," Natalie says. "You don't need me there. Just saying."

The beautiful brick buildings of Camden College tower over the street as they ride at a leisurely pace through the campus. They pass the building where Rock taught his classes, the building Brett has spent so much time in. Memories of her father flood into her mind. She pushes them into the inner recesses, trying not to focus on sentimentality. She needs her mind focused on the task at hand: locating the other cities and finding Esteban. Only then will she allow herself to reminisce about the joyous past.

* * * * *

Dr. Brown isn't home yet. While they wait in the kitchen, Brett walks over to the bay window that overlooks the side yard. A group of children are playing on the sidewalk. She stares past them intently, looking for a sign of a black sedan. She still has an uneasy feeling that the men from the Department of Antiquity are out there somewhere. Sims followed her right to the city, and he had entered before her. Brett is sure that the men from the government who drove around in unmarked cars were still looking for her dad's book.

She touches the square shape in her side pocket. Natalie steps up beside her and peers through the window. "You don't think those guys are still out there, do you?" Brett keeps her eyes fixed on the kids bounding down the roadway.

"I would bet they are out there waiting."

Natalie grimaces. "That's not good."

"No, it isn't," Brett says. "This time we won't let them follow us."

"How are we going to do that?"

"Not sure, but we will think of something."

Brett walks over and sits down at the round kitchen table. She gently pulls the book out of her pocket and holds it tightly in her hands, then places it delicately on the kitchen table. Natalie walks over and stands beside her. "You think that will tell us how to find the other cities?"

Brett nods her head. "I'm confident." She runs her fingers along the faded brown spine of the weathered book. Her breath catches in her throat as she slowly opens the cover. The yellowed pages feel rough against her fingers.

She looks at the neat, slanted writing that fills the pages. Her father's orderly handwriting. Brett has spent enormous amounts of time in the past days perusing the book for any bits of information that could help her. Finally, she has new information; it's time to consult the field journal for answers.

She skims the section with the maps of New Mexico. The routes of Coronado and Esteban are drawn on the faded pages. Her finger traces the line representing Esteban. "Where are you?" she says softly. She looks up and stares off into the distance. Her thoughts wander to the canyon where she saw the city two weeks ago. "This map isn't going to help this time," she whispers. "There has to be something in here."

Brett turns the pages faster and faster, searching for other phrases that mention Esteban, but not a single page contains a reference to him ever visiting another city. The frustration builds inside her. Brett grits her teeth so tightly that her jaw aches. She presses her right hand against her head, trying to force an answer to materialize from nothingness. "You okay?" Natalie asks.

Brett blinks rapidly and slowly returns her gaze to the book. "Yeah, no worries."

The sound of a car brings both girls leaping out of their chairs and hurrying to the window. Dr. Brown's Ford Escape rolls to a stop in the driveway. "Just mom," Natalie says. Brett walks back over to the kitchen table, where the journal is still open. She places her hands in her pockets and begins walking in circles around the table, looking down at the book with each pass, hoping that some new bit of information will present itself.

"Is that helping any?" Natalie asks.

Brett looks at her with narrowed eyes. Natalie smiles broadly. "Thought you might need a little tension release." Brett sits in the chair, and her head thuds onto the table.

"It's not here," she says through a muffled voice. She can feel Natalie sit across from her, but her head remains encircled by her arms.

"We will find it," Natalie says, a little too enthusiastically. Brett rolls her head until she can see the face of her best friend beaming at her.

"It's not going to be as easy this time."

"This time?" Natalie says. "I don't think last time was all that easy."

"Everything was in here." Brett says holding up the book.

"Yes, but it wasn't easy," Natalie replies. "I nearly fell into a ravine that would have been certain death."

Brett didn't want to think about that part of the trip. She starts to reply when the door opens and Dr. Brown walks into the room. A look of deep concern clouds her face as she looks at both girls. She places her bag on the floor and closes the door without looking away from either one of them. "It is good to see you, Brett," she says. "How have you been?"

Brett hasn't been over to Natalie's house since they returned home from New Mexico. Brett and Natalie haven't been apart since they returned, but they have tried to give Natalie's mom a little more time to deal with all that has happened. "Been staying busy," Brett says.

Dr. Brown motions toward the book. "I can see that."

She picks up a glass from the counter and fills it at the sink. Brett can see her hand shaking as she brings the cup up to her lips. "Dr. Brown," she says delicately, "I wouldn't be here if I didn't need your help." Dr. Brown's eyes go wide. The cup rattles violently as she places it on the counter. "I'm not expecting you to go this time," Brett says calmly. "I just need your assistance and that is it. No trips. No danger. I promise."

Dr. Brown looks at Natalie. The concern on her face is revealed through the lines that crease the skin around her eyes. Natalie starts to protest, but Dr. Brown stops he with a gesture. She sits down across the table from Brett and Natalie, her eyes distant. "What do you need?" she asks.

"We saw Dr. Mies today," Brett starts.

"Was he able to help?"

"Not much. But he did tell us something extraordinary."

Dr. Brown glances at Natalie with a look that says, "I can't believe you went over to see him." Natalie glares back at her mother.

"He told us that Esteban wasn't in Cibola." Brett waits for this information to register before she continues. Dr. Brown doesn't take her eyes off Natalie. "He said that Esteban had moved onto one of the other cities." Brett pauses, waiting for Dr. Brown to say something. Dr. Brown glances over at Brett before placing her hands on the table and shaking her head.

"Why would you bother him?" she says harshly. "Dr. Mies has been through a terrible ordeal, and he doesn't need to relive it again and again."

Natalie gets up quickly, rocking the table with her legs. She stands with her hands clenched in fists so tight that her fingers turn white. Brett holds up her hand, hoping to stop Natalie from exploding, but Natalie doesn't notice. "Brett needs the information if she hopes to ever find her dad," she says, her voice quivering. "And we need your help too."

Dr. Brown shakes her head. "We aren't risking our lives this time," she says forcefully. She looks at Natalie. "Not again."

Natalie stomps her foot down hard on the floor. "I'm going with her wherever Brett goes," she says as tears form in her eyes. "We agreed on the way home that we would try. You're not breaking your promise."

Dr. Brown shakes her head and looks toward the door. "We don't know if others like Sims are looking for that thing," she says, motioning toward the book. "Ever since they dropped that off at my office bad things have happened. I don't want them to continue." Brett looks down at the withered yellow pages of the book, at the handwriting of her father.

"Dr. Brown," she says, not looking away from the book, "this book helped us find Cibola. We were so close to getting my dad out of there." She looks up at Dr. Brown, her blue eyes dancing. "I am going to use this to find him again, but I need your help to do that. I'm not asking you to go with me. I'm just asking for a little expert advice."

Brett stares up at her with eyes that shine like beacons in the dimly lit kitchen. She can feel the energy pulsing through her with every beat of her heart. Dr. Brown glances at Natalie, then her shoulders slump forward and she lowers her hand. "How can I help?" Brett glances at Natalie and smiles. Natalie looks at her mom and slowly takes a seat as Brett continues.

"Dr. Mies says there are other cities. I am wondering, could we use the electroscope to find them just like we did to find Cibola?"

Dr. Brown closes her eyes and begins tapping on the table, as she always does when in deep thought. The tapping is rhythmic; Brett can make out a tune, but it isn't one that she has heard before. Suddenly, Dr. Brown's eyes open. "I don't think so," she says. Brett shakes her head at the answer. "Look," Dr. Brown says, "we had an approximate location of Cibola when we went to New Mexico. Rock had figured that part out. The city would appear along this trend line over a given period of hours." She points at an area of the map.

"So, you think it is impossible to find the others? Brett asks.

"Not impossible. But without a starting point, we would be stumbling around just hoping we hit it."

"The magnetic anomalies can be used though?"

"Of course. We just need a point in space to start from."

Dr. Brown touches the map that shows the routes of Esteban and Coronado. "Both of these have starting points in space. Rock realized that if he followed the route from this starting point, the anomaly should increase in intensity the closer he was to the city. And he was right. We found it." Dr. Brown looks up and her eyes widen. "Now, are there any other maps or descriptions that describe other points in space?"

Brett looks down at the map. She knows the answer to the question. She examines the book for hours every day searching for answers. Another map of another area isn't in her dad's journal. He had focused his energy and effort on finding Cibola. The other cities, if he knew about them, are not even mentioned in the field book.

Brett runs her hands through her blonde hair as she grits her teeth. The field book is useless now. How is she going to find the city where her father is? How is she going to find Esteban? She looks up at Dr. Brown. "There isn't another map," she says slowly. Dr. Brown places her hand on Brett's shoulder. Brett slowly closes the book and shoves it into her side pocket.

The book has helped her along this journey so many times. It is the piece of her father that has seemed to whisper to her out of the abyss. It has pointed her in the right direction time and again. Now, she is left alone. Her father can't help her any longer. The words of the diary were written specifically for one city, and that city is now unavailable for the next two hundred years or so.

Brett's mind is slow and plodding as she tries to figure out what to do. "Brett," Natalie calls. "Brett." Brett looks up at her. Natalie tries to smile, but her lips don't work correctly and it looks like a weird grimace. "We will figure this out."

Brett looks at Dr. Brown. "There has to be something we can do."

Dr. Brown shakes her head. "It will be tough to find the starting point. That bit of information is vital to finding the magnetic anomalies that are hiding the entrances to the city."

Brett looks back at the table, trying to think of some way she can solve this new problem—trying to view it like any other problem she has been given. She can hear the words of her dad echoing in her head. "What does the data tell you?" The data tells her that there is no possible way to find the point in space from which to measure. Her faith in her ability begins to wain as she sits at the kitchen table. She can hear deep breaths from Natalie and her mom. Finally, Brett stands up. "Thank you, Dr. Brown," she says softly, "I appreciate all your help." She walks toward the door.

"I'm sorry I can't do more," Dr. Brown says.

Brett turns and smiles at her. "You have done more than enough." Natalie is sitting at the table, still staring at her. She has never seen Natalie without something to say. For the first time, Natalie is speechless. "See you tomorrow," Brett says as she grabs the cold handle of the door. She turns the knob and steps out into the thick air of Camden. She pulls the door closed and stands still, contemplating her next move. The humid air seems to press on her like a vice. It squeezes her lungs as she takes in deep breaths. "What am I going to do?" she asks as she steps off the porch and walks toward her bike.

CHAPTER 3

Rays of Hope

It has been a week since Brett visited Dr. Brown, and her disappointment at her failure is still fresh and raw. It still gnaws at her insides like a dog would a bone. The first three days were horrible. She had tried reading her dad's book again and again. She had become so angry that she threw the book against the wall so hard it took out a chunk of plaster.

Brett wakes on Friday. Her legs dangle off the bed as she stares out the window toward the early morning sky. The black and purple backdrop of space is filled with thousands of tiny sparkles of light. The lights pulse rhythmically, as if a tune is playing somewhere in the recesses of space.

She has anguished over her talk with Dr. Brown; her mind has become clouded with the enormity of the task at hand. How is she going to find the other cities when she doesn't know where to start? How is she going to protect cities that she cannot locate? The Spanish sentry of Cibola never told her how to find them and protect them. She pushes the palms of her hands against her eyes. This is a problem that she needs to solve. But how? As the time ticks away on the clock, and no answers manifest themselves and the journal does not give any answers, she decides to clear her mind of it for the moment. She decides that after what seems like a million tries and failures, she needs to take a step back from the hunt—to take some time away from the diary to think. She is going to focus on the farm and her chores, and maybe if she isn't actively seeking answers, they will come to her. Her dad once told her, "An overworked mind sometimes can't find acceptable solutions." She decides to trust in his words.

Brett places her feet on the floor and quickly walks across the dimly lit room to an old, faded chair that sits in front of a matching dresser. Her blue jeans are draped over the back along with a dull blue and black checkered shirt. She quickly dresses and slips on a pair of work boots that have patches of leather missing on the toe. She quietly walks across the unfinished wooden floor and slowly pulls her bedroom door open. She doesn't want to wake Grandpa Jake at five-thirty in the morning. The door creaks loudly. Brett stops, listening intently for a sound from Grandpa Jake's room. She stands motionless for a few seconds. Finally, satisfied that the creaking door hasn't caused him to wake, she tiptoes lightly down the hallway toward the stairs.

Brett walks by Grandpa Jake's bedroom door and again stops to listen for any sound coming from the other side of the door. As she looks at the door, her mind drifts back to a few months ago when the man from the Department of Antiquity was holding him captive. Her heart begins to race as she remembers the fight with the man, and how Natalie had knocked him out. A smile spreads across her face as she sees the image of Natalie sitting on the crumbled mass of the man.

After a few seconds of careful listening, Brett creeps down the hallway and begins her descent down the stairs. She steps over the step that always creaks loudly. She lets out a deep breath as she makes it to the living room. She didn't wake up Grandpa Jake, which is a good thing.

She turns toward the door and starts toward it. The silence is broken by the sound of someone clearing their throat. Fear grips her and she turns around quickly, her hands out in front of her ready for whoever is in the room with her. "Not going to fight me?" a raspy voice says from the darkness. Brett relaxes as Grandpa Jake hobbles into the room from the kitchen.

"No sir."

"You're up awfully early," he says with narrowed eyes.

"Yeah. I wanted to get a head start on my chores."

"I see," he says softly. "Before you get out there and get started you should get some breakfast."

Grandpa Jake turns and limps into the kitchen. Brett wants to get started, but she decides that something to eat sounds good. She stuffs her hands into her pockets and walks into the kitchen. There on the table are biscuits piled high on a plate with containers of honey and jelly in mason jars. Grandpa Jake always enjoys canning the food that he grows, and Brett enjoys eating it.

Brett smells the sweet fragrance of the biscuits as she sits down across from Grandpa Jake. He sits motionless, watching her as she grabs two biscuits and rips the tops off of them. Puffs of white steam slowly rise from the white bread. She quickly grabs a knife and scoops up some butter from the flower-blazoned dish. Brett likes to see the butter melt on the biscuit, adding sweetness to the delectable bread.

The butter melts instantly, and Brett places the top on the biscuit and takes a hurried bite. The soft, flaky bread almost dissolves in her mouth. She takes another bite without fully swallowing the first. Her cheeks are full, and she glances up at Grandpa Jake. He looks at her in disbelief. "Sorry," she says as crumbs fall from her mouth. "I must have been hungrier than I thought." She gulps down the rest and lets out a slight cough.

"I haven't seen you eat like this in a long while," he says.

"It could be the cooking," she says smiling. "This stuff is the best."

Grandpa Jake grits his teeth and rubs his chin. Brett can hear the scraping of his pale, thin fingers against the stubble. She knows this look all too well. This is the concerned Grandpa Jake. The one that is going to try to help her even when there is nothing he can do. She waits patiently for him to find the words he wants to use. She stares down at her plate and absentmindedly breaks off a piece of the soft biscuit and places it in her mouth.

"Dr. Brown called," he says. "She asked how you were."

Brett glances up. "Why?"

Jake leans back in his chair with his right hand caressing his chin. He studies her for a few seconds. "Natalie said you have been too busy to see her." He watches her intently. She looks away from his penetrating stare.

"I have been busy," she says. "Need to get things in order around here."

Grandpa Jake scratches his neck slowly. "They are worried about you," he says. "I'm worried." She smiles at him, trying to ease his mind.

"Grandpa, we have seen things that are weird. We saw Cibola. We almost found Dad. We were told that we had to protect the other cities, and that bit is really strange." She blinks her eyes slowly. "I tried to find it, believe me, but I can't. I can't figure this one out. The journal doesn't have anything in it about the six other cities."

Her shoulders slump forward. She can feel the weight of her failure pressing down on her. It binds her chest, and she feels as though her blood is pumping in slow motion. She looks up at him, her eyes wide. "I need a break from it. I need a chance to clear my mind."

"So that is why you have been working from sunup to sundown?"

"Sorry, Grandpa," she responds. "That is the only thing that helps."

"I knew it."

"Not sure how long I need to do this, but I will do it as long as I need to."

He grimaces again. Brett can see the pain in his eyes as he searches for a soothing word. A word of comfort. She stands up and brushes the crumbs from her hands onto the plate. "I need to get going," she says. She takes the plate over to the sink and washes it quickly. She places the dish on the drying rack and walks toward the door without looking back.

"I need to go over to your dad's place today to get and a few things," he says. "I would like for you to go with me."

Brett stops, her hands are resting on her hips. She really would like to see her house again. It has been months since she has been there. How could it hurt? It might help to clear her mind even further so that she could locate the answer to the riddle. "After work," she says without turning around.

"After work," Grandpa Jake replies. Brett walks out of the kitchen with her heart racing for some unknown reason.

* * * * *

Brett is sweaty when she runs into the house at six o'clock. The heat of the afternoon and the trimming of hooves and building new stalls in the barn made the last two hours fly by. Brett has spent four hours working after she took the middle of the day off to read and relax in her hammock. Her clothes are wet and sticking to her body as she rushes toward the steps. Grandpa Jake is sitting at the kitchen table. He looks up at her as she readies to bound up the stairs. "I'm going to take a quick shower and then we can go," she says. He nods slowly.

She races up the steps two at a time and throws open her door. She hurries to find her favorite pair of cargo pants and a red checkered shirt. She walks across the hall into the bathroom. She showers quickly and returns to her room with wet hair that drips down onto her shirt and pants, leaving dark splotches on the fabric. She slips her hiking boots on and grabs her dad's field book. She doesn't know why she picks it up. Maybe it is out of habit, or maybe she will need it. She shoves the tattered brown book into the side pocket of her pants and walks out of her tidy room.

As she walks down the steps, she can see that Grandpa Jake is standing at the table. He is twirling his keys in his calloused hand. "You ready?" he asks. She gives him a thumbs up and steps down the stairs. He hobbles toward the door and Brett follows close behind him. He opens the door and gingerly steps out onto the porch and takes slow, careful steps down the wooden steps. Brett closes the door behind her and walks after him with her hands deep in her pockets. Her mind wanders to what her old room looks like now. Has it changed as her life has changed? She has a hard time remembering what it looks like. The wall color, the posters on the wall, and the smell of the room are distant as she tries to recall them.

She walks around the old red Ford pickup truck with its rusty fenders and peeling paint. This is a work truck and Grandpa always makes sure he tells everyone that is its role. The door lets out a loud creak as she opens it. She climbs up onto the bench seat that seems way too long to fit in a truck and closes the door. The loud squeak of the door is much louder when being closed than being opened. She buckles the loose seatbelt and looks out the window toward the barn. The goats are bounding around in the field. A smile crosses her face as she watches Julie and Heather jump and dart at each other. They bring her happiness and make her laugh every day, and the more time she spends with them the more she craves their company.

The truck shakes and rumbles as Grandpa Jake starts it. The motion from the engine causes the cab to rock and sway. She looks at Grandpa Jake. "It will be good to go home," she says. "I miss my bed." That is something that she does remember. The soft feather pillows and the fluffy pillowtop mattress. She has to admit that her sleep hasn't been regular since her dad disappeared, and she doubts that it would have been any different even if she was sleeping in her old bed. All the same, she does miss the way her mattress and pillow envelop her body.

Grandpa Jake puts the truck in gear. It lurches forward and the engine struggles to continue, yet they start moving down the gravel driveway all the same. Brett rolls the window down and places her right arm on the frame, staring out at the fading sunlight as it creeps lower and lower over the tree line. The bright oranges and yellows in the sky cast a vibrant picture over a canvas of pale blue. She lets out a deep breath and leans back in her seat, enjoying the breeze in her face and the smell of late summer.

* * * * *

Brett stares out the window as Grandpa Jake puts the truck in park. The two-story brick house is lifeless as the last rays of sunlight radiate around the shingles on the roof. The curtains are closed and darkness envelopes the porch. She stares up toward the window on the right side of the house. That is her room up there. Brett remembers having the window open during the summer while listening to a Kansas City Royals game on the radio. It seems like a lifetime ago.

She opens the door and it emits a slow, loud creak. Her eyes never leave her old home. She hasn't been here since the day after her dad disappeared, and she can feel the heaviness of the air as she places her feet on the broken concrete driveway. She walks down the driveway and starts up the S-shaped walkway toward the porch. Her mind is slow and lethargic as she steps up the creaking boards of the old house. She can hear the plodding steps of her grandpa behind her as she stands staring at the door. The cicadas are chirping loudly in the warm night air as she waits for something to happen.

She expects her dad to come bounding out of the house and pick her up in his arms and squeeze her in a bone-crunching hug. Maybe the last few months never truly happened. Maybe they are a figment of her active imagination. Suddenly, she is thrust back into reality. "Stay alert," Jake whispers. "You never know what might happen."

Brett's pulse quickens until her heart threatens to burst out of her chest. She looks up at the windows, searching for any signs of movement from the curtains. They remain still as Grandpa Jake removes his key from his pocket and places it in the lock. The lock disengages with a loud *thunk*, and Jake slowly opens the heavy wooden door. Brett stands behind him, holding her breath and straining her ears for any unusual sound. The only sound is that of the cicadas.

Brett follows Grandpa Jake into the dark living room of the house. He finds the switch and turns on the light. The white light from the fluorescent bulbs fills the narrow room. The brown leather couch and chair are covered by a film of dust, which is not normal. Her dad always kept the house clean and tidy. Finding dust on everything makes Brett feel the need to clean.

She steps around Grandpa Jake and walks toward the stairway that leads to the second floor. She wants to see her room. There is comfort in being back where she has spent so much time. Grandpa Jake grabs her arm. "Keep your eyes and ears open," he whispers. She nods as she walks behind the dusty couch toward the paneled staircase. There are pictures on the wall of her and her dad standing on the edge of a rock pillar at Badlands National Park. They are both smiling at the camera. Brett has her Royals hat pulled down over her eyes and her dad has his wide-brimmed hat sitting high atop his head. There is another picture of a slender, blonde-haired woman with glasses standing on the same pillar.

Brett stops and stares at the pictures absently. She has seen the photographs hundreds of times as she walked up to her room, but this time she studies them with intense curiosity. Her mom stares out at her from the picture with a soft smile on her face. How she misses seeing her, talking to her. She fights back the raw emotions that flood her mind and shakes her head. "Stay focused," she tells herself. She walks up the wooden steps as the boards moan in displeasure.

She makes it to the top of the stairs and stands motionless, listening. The upstairs is just as quiet as the downstairs, and after a few tense seconds, she walks down the hallway toward her room. It is dark, and the farther she goes the more she feels that she should have turned on the light. She walks by her dad's bedroom door, then his office door, and finally comes to the dark, stained-oak door that leads to her room.

She reaches out toward the handle. Her right hand trembles slightly as she grasps the silver-plated knob. Her breath catches in her throat as she turns the handle and slowly pushes the door open. She isn't sure what to expect. Maybe one of the men that followed her a few months ago might jump out at her and force her to give them the diary. She shakes her head. "That is silly. They are already in Cibola. They beat me to the city." She turns the lights on, and a bright yellow light fills the room.

On the dull gray walls, there are pictures of rocks, fossils, and dinosaurs. The bed is made, with her comforter pulled tight on the corners creating a very crisp look. She walks over to the antique writing desk that sits next to the window. She studies it carefully. "That's odd." The dust on the desk has an outline of where her books were once positioned. Now they are on the other side of the desk. She runs her finger through the dust as she thinks quickly. "Someone has been here—recently."

Her heart races as she backs away. Tiny droplets of sweat begin forming on the back of her neck as she stares at the desk. Her mind works quickly on analyzing the data in front of her. "They were looking for this," she says, softly patting the side of her leg with her hand. The field book fits snugly in the pocket of her cargo pants.

She looks around at the other objects in the room. The books on the bookshelf are not in the specific locations where she had them placed. They are no longer positioned neatly on the shelf. Some of the books have been pulled out, revealing the covers. She turns around quickly and walks swiftly from the room. Her fast footfalls echo throughout the upstairs.

She stops abruptly at her dad's office door. "I bet they searched in here too." She reaches out for the silver door handle and notices that her hand is shaking violently. Brett opens and closes her hand, trying to control the tremors that are pulsing through the skin. She grasps the cold metal of the knob and carefully turns it. The door creaks faintly as she pushes it open. She holds her breath as she lets the door swing inward.

Brett stares into the black room. She strains her eyes trying to pick up any movement—or anyone that might be lurking in the shadows. A clock ticks somewhere in the office, sending chill bumps rushing to the surface of her skin. She strains her ears for any sound that someone in the room might make, but the only sounds are the repetitive ticking of the clock and the loud beating of her heart. She takes a deep breath and decides it is time to check inside the room.

She stealthily moves through the opening and crouches down slightly. She reaches her trembling finger toward the light switch and flips it on quickly. The yellow light illuminates the room and spills out into the hallway. Brett peers around the room, certain that someone is waiting for her. She scans the four corners from the relative safety of the hallway. There isn't anyone inside. The breath that Brett has been holding in rushes from her lungs and into the air.

She walks in and immediately starts investigating the positions of her dad's papers, which are in neat piles on top of a metal desk. The papers are in order, right where he always keeps them. She checks the drawers. All of them are ajar. This isn't the way her dad leaves his office. The drawers are always closed tightly. Someone has searched the compartments of the desk. This isn't good.

Brett opens the top left drawer and sorts through the papers. There are just sketches of rock outcrops and strike and dip markings for some geologic structures in Camden. She has taken hundreds of strike and dip readings with her dad around town. Finding this document presses her desire to find her dad back to the forefront of her consciousness. She has done a good job of focusing on other things beside the diary and the lost cities, and she has closed her mind to her failure at trying to find another way into the golden cities. Finding this drawing causes her face to flush. The fear has ebbed in her body as she stares at the drawing, and new confidence builds inside of her.

The top right drawer holds other documents about geology. She tries the lower left drawer. It is heavier and doesn't open as easily, and no wonder. She looks down at six rocks with white chalk written on them. Brett can make out the sweeping scrawl of her father's hand. Sandstone, dolomite, shale, limestone, chert nodule, and brachiopod. She pushes the drawer closed with a bit of effort.

She pulls on the final drawer with enough force that it nearly falls onto the floor. She catches the wooden box and places it on the desk, rifling through the papers inside. She is not sure what she is looking for, but she is sure she will recognize it when she sees it. Paper after paper passes through her hands, all just more scientific studies of the rock structure in and around Camden. She takes her hand out of the drawer and looks down at the desk. The room has been searched.

Maybe the people that broke into the house found something.

Brett lets out a deep breath. Her heart rate slows, and calmness returns to her. "They are probably gone, so no need to worry about them jumping out at me," she says as she reaches her hand up to her chin. "I don't remember dad ever talking about anything else but Cibola, and all that information is in the field book." She leans back in the desk chair with her hands behind her head and stares up at the paneled ceiling. "They were looking for the book," she says. "That has to be it."

She sits up and grabs the still-open bottom drawer. She pushes it in, but it stops about an inch from closing entirely. She absentmindedly opens it and tries closing it again. The drawer will not close. She opens the drawer and leans down so that her face is inches from the opening. She peers inside, examining the dark recesses. Nothing is sticking out that can keep it from closing all the way. She tries once more. This time her face is next to the drawer as she slowly closes it. She peers inside as the drawer closes. Once again it stops abruptly.

Brett stares into the darkness with her eyes narrowed. She pulls the drawer open wider and slowly moves her hand into the space behind the drawer. There isn't anything impeding its progress. She squints and moves her arm deeper, and just as she reaches the back part of the cabinet, she feels a small bunch of stacked papers. Her fingers fumble across the first page, then the second. She grabs them and slowly pulls them up over the drawer.

Brett has five wrinkled papers in her hand. She lays them on the wooden desk and tries to smooth out the curved edges. She pushes the drawer in and this time it closes securely. She looks intently at the first yellowed sheet. There on the page in dark ink is a sweeping, majestic handwritten note with carefully formed arches and loops that form beautiful letters. This isn't her dad's handwriting, as his letters are coarse and difficult to decipher. She takes the top page off the desk and stares at the magnificent writing. "J. Ortiz explored large portions of what is now the southeastern part of A. Saw glittering walled structures in the distance as he traveled down the great river." The passage continues detailing the travels of Ortiz and his journey up the river toward the vibrant city. "It shines like the light that passes through diamonds, and my excitement is evident to my native companions. They have said the people that dwell in the city are fierce warriors. But I will not fear."

Brett finds that she has been holding her breath as she reads. "What is this?" she asks out loud. She falls into the chair and lays the first page aside. She picks up the second page; it is written in the same looping hand. "The river seems to go on forever, and we are starting to run low on provisions. My companions tell me that we must turn toward the rising sun to find the gated entrance."

Brett places the paper on the desk and stares up at the ceiling. "This sounds just like Esteban's story," she says. "What if this guy Ortiz found one of the other cities?" Her heart starts beating faster and faster as she thinks about the prospect of having a location to start from. "He is going up a great river. Maybe that is the Mississippi," she says. "He must turn toward the rising sun. That would take him east." A smile spreads across her face as the excitement builds inside her. This is it. This is the start of the hunt. Where will this take her? She isn't quite sure but her mind wanders to the spot Ortiz is describing. She can see herself in a flat-bottom boat or a canoe paddling up the river in search of another city.

Brett grabs the pages and holds them tightly in her hands. Her mind remains fixed on the opportunity of finding a way to her dad, and she doesn't notice the door opening slowly. The clock on the walls ticks loudly and the chimes begin signifying that it is now nine o'clock. She glances toward the moving door and jumps in fright. Grandpa Jake is standing in the doorway looking at her.

"I heard voices," he says.

Brett has the papers held tightly in her hand. She scowls at him. "Don't do that, Grandpa," she says. "You scared me to death." He walks into the room, looks around, and sees the papers in her hand. "Someone has been here," Brett says.

He stares at her with his wide eyes. "How do you know?" he asks.

Brett walks around the desk and moves swiftly toward the hallway. She peers down the corridor. "My books and papers have been moved, and whoever came here didn't close the drawers in the desk." She turns and looks at him sternly. "But they didn't find these." She holds up the papers and a smile spreads across her face. "I think we can find Dad, Grandpa," she says. "I am sure of it."

CHAPTER 4

Mysterious Author

Brett stands in her bedroom with the pages spread out on her bed. She has her hands on her hips and her Royals hat pulled down close to her eyes. The volume on the radio is low, and the words of the announcer flow from the speaker. "Salvador Perez up here in the eighth. Looking for something he can pull so those runners on second and third can score." Brett taps her foot rhythmically as the crowd cheers. Listening to Royals games always helps her focus and get her ready for the start of an investigation. "Here's the pitch . . . and it's in play down the third-base line. This should score Merrifield and Dozier."

Brett taps her foot on the wooden floorboards in response to the cheer of the crowd. She stares down at the yellowed papers, thinking about the clues they have provided. Ortiz references a place on a great river called Pacaha. She has never heard that name before, and she makes a mental note to research that particular location. If the great river is the Mississippi River, that name should be easy to find. It could be a city along the river, but she isn't sure.

The writings also say that Ortiz ventured east, away from the setting sun, as he journeyed up the river. That would put the sighting of the city somewhere in eastern Tennessee or Mississippi. She narrows her eyes as she scrutinizes the carefully handwritten notes on the fourth page. Gausili appears to be an important point in the Ortiz route. Brett still doesn't know where Gausili is when focusing on the great river, but it could be on another river east of the Mississippi.

The flowing letters of the handwritten note loop and curl across the page. Brett pushes her hat back and rubs her forehead. "Who wrote all these notes?" she asks. She is genuinely curious about the level of detail. The author must have conducted months if not years of research to piece together the story of this man Ortiz. Brett believed that based on the style and structure of the letters, the author had to be a female. This is something else that she will need to solve if she ever hopes to find her dad. Maybe the author of these pages can help her locate another entrance to the cities of gold.

There is a knock at the door. She remains rooted in her spot, glaring at the brittle pages. Grandpa Jake opens the door. "It's getting late," he says.

"I'm sorry Grandpa. I am still trying to figure this out."

"Might need to sleep on it."

She picks up one of the pages and turns toward her grandfather. She holds the wrinkled paper up so that he can see it. "Do you recognize this writing?"

He leans his head back and blinks his eyes quickly as he tries to focus on the letters. "I don't think so," he says.

"You ever heard of Gausili?"

He blinks at her and tilts his head to the right. "You know better than to ask me something like that," he says. She turns and walks to her writing desk.

The announcer on the radio yells, "Royals win! Wow! What a game." Brett opens her laptop and begins pressing the keys.

"Brett, it is almost eleven," Grandpa Jake says. "We can pick this up tomorrow." She ignores him and types in the word *Gausili*. She taps the enter button. Instantly a picture of Hernando de Soto appears on the screen: a bearded man with dark eyes and a face filled with cheerful optimism. She clicks on the link and is taken to a description of the expedition conducted by de Soto. He had explored the southeastern part of what is now the United States in search of gold.

Gausili is a city that de Soto visited, located in the mountains of what is now eastern Tennessee. Her blood pumps wildly as this new bit of information fills her mind. Could de Soto have done in the east what Coronado was doing in the west? If that is the case, this city of Gausili could be the starting point for finding it. She stares at the screen, her mind working to piece together the route and the connection to Cibola. How would she find this place without a map to guide her? The answer comes to her quickly. "I will need to create the map."

Brett quickly becomes lost in the process of how she will make a map that will guide her. There is so much that she doesn't know . . . how is she going to collect all this information quickly? She bites her lip as she fights back the fear of not being able to figure out how to help her dad. She has been fighting this battle since she returned from New Mexico. Thinking about what she needs to do brings her past failures flooding back into her mind.

She grits her teeth and decides she will not allow the fear to possess her. She looks up at Grandpa Jake. "I'm going over to Camden tomorrow," she says. "I need to talk to someone about de Soto and the city of Gausili." Grandpa Jake crosses his arms as he always does when he is ready to argue against something, but this time a twinkle of light sparkles in his eyes.

"First thing in the morning," he replies without a smile.

"First thing," Brett says, nodding.

* * * * *

The bright orange light from the sunrise filters into Brett's room as she hurriedly pulls on her boots and ties them. She didn't sleep much last night, as she spent hours thinking about de Soto, Ortiz, and Gausili. She has never heard of Ortiz or Gausili before, but de Soto is someone that she learned about in elementary school. The journey he took through the South to find a depository of gold has been well studied. However, the mystery of where he went along the way and where he was buried still baffles scholars.

Brett stands up and presses the wrinkles out of her khaki cargo pants. She grabs her dad's field book from the desk and places it in her pocket, then she takes her own dull orange field book off the bookshelf and walks toward the door. She will start a new log with all the information she can gather from the historians at Camden College.

Brett bounds down the steps two at a time, jumps down the final few steps, and lands in the living room with a loud *thud*. She walks quickly into the kitchen. Grandpa Jake looks up at her as he drinks from a steaming cup, his bright eyes dancing through the haze of steam as she sits down across from him. He keeps his eyes upon her as she grabs a biscuit and stuffs the whole thing in her mouth. She chews fast, ready to be on her way. "You can take your time" he says. Brett doesn't look up. She grabs another biscuit as she swallows the first one. Grandpa Jake laughs. "I checked Dr. Hall's office hours for today," he says from behind his steaming coffee cup. "We have an hour."

Brett looks down at the soft, fluffy bread in her hands. She takes a small bite. She is ready to start this journey now, but she has to wait another hour for it to begin. "Okay, Grandpa," she says. She stares at her plate, rehearsing what she will ask Dr. Hall when she meets her. Brett has a list of about forty questions that sit on the edge of her mind, and she is sure she will ask all of them. *Where is Gausili? Why is it important? Who is Ortiz? Did Ortiz guide de Soto? Could de Soto's quest have ended with him finding a golden city?*

Her heart begins to beat faster and faster as she anticipates the answers to her questions. She can feel the heat rising in her face as her very own quest is ready to begin. Her mind wanders back to the beautiful handwritten note that she found inside her dad's desk. "Who wrote it?" she asks as her eyes stare into the vacancy of space. She mindlessly takes another bite as she ponders the identity of the mysterious author.

Whoever the author is, they have given her a lifeline. They are directing her path toward the cities that she has been charged with protecting. The author is also guiding her path to the location of her father, and that is the most important part of the journey. Brett knows he is alive, and she knows he is out in the haze, not visible from this world at the moment. She will pull the veil down between the two worlds very soon, and with Dr. Hall's help, that time is closer than it has been in quite a while.

CHAPTER 5

De Soto's Path

The truck rocks as Grandpa Jake drives the old pickup down the treelined streets of Camden College. They pass the brick building where her father taught his classes in mineralogy and sedimentation. She has listened to many of his lectures through the years. She always found it fascinating the way that minerals orient themselves based on the polarity of the earth.

She likes identifying minerals and rocks. Brett always joined in the lessons as Rock taught his students. She found it gratifying when she could solve a problem before they could. Rock taught them how to figure out what minerals are in the rocks. "What does the rock say to you?" he would always ask. His students would look at him like he was from a distant planet, but Brett realized it was his way of getting students to think. Her dad never gave answers freely. He always made you work for them.

The truck turns left into the parking lot of a three-story brick building. The sign at the entrance to the parking lot reads "Holt Hall." Holt Hall is the building where the history, archaeology, and anthropological studies departments are located. Brett has driven her bike by this building hundreds of times, but she has never ventured inside. Anthropology never really interested her. She didn't like studying how societies or cultures formed.

The archaeology side she found quite interesting. Her father had introduced her to the novels of Indiana Jones, and she was hooked from the first word of the *Peril at Delphi*. Finding something that had been hidden for hundreds or thousands of years resonated with her. She had heard a story where archeologists found a whole city in Guatemala using satellite imagery. Finding something like that would be remarkable. Brett still has the desire to seek out the truths of the distant past.

The history department isn't as glamourous as geology or archeology, but she found that the research side of history paired well with the sciences she enjoys. Science is research-oriented, and treasure hunting is mostly researching before you ever go outside in search of hidden artifacts. You always need an "X" that marks the spot, and the only way to locate it is through weeks and weeks of painstaking research.

Brett started researching the route of de Soto last night. After Grandpa Jake went to bed, she found a map by Charles Hudson that presumably traced the route de Soto took through the southeast. De Soto started in the Tampa, Florida area and moved northward into the areas now known as Georgia, South Carolina, and Tennessee. Brett drew the entire map in her field book. She noted the different locations with modern-day cities penciled into the drawing. Brett also labeled the native cities in large block letters.

Brett has pages of notes on the path and the people that de Soto encountered, but there is plenty of information still to find. That is why they are parked outside Holt Hall. Brett opens the door and jumps out of the truck. As she closes the door, a loud voice calls from behind her: "Thought you would do this without me?" Brett turns. Natalie is standing with her feet set firmly on the concrete sidewalk. Her hands are planted onto her hips. She scowls at Brett.

"Yeah . . . sorry about that," Brett responds.

"We are a team, you know."

"I know."

"I won't hold it against you," Natalie says. "Thanks, Grandpa Jake, for giving me a heads up on what is going on."

Grandpa Jake hobbles slowly around the car. "Figured you would want to be here," he says.

Brett glances at Natalie with a look that says, "I am sorry for not calling." Natalie turns and starts walking toward the dark glass door at the entrance. "Let's get this show on the road. We have a city to find."

Brett looks over at Grandpa Jake as they step up on the sidewalk. "Thanks," she says.

He opens his mouth to respond, but Natalie hollers from the glass door that she has already opened, "Let's go. Discoveries wait for no one." Grandpa Jake grimaces and he shakes his head as they get closer to the door.

"You called her," Brett says with a smile.

"Yeah . . . starting to rethink that."

Natalie holds the heavy door open and stands waiting for Grandpa Jake and Brett to arrive. She taps her foot as they take the last step up to the concrete landing. "I heard that," Natalie says. "But I know that you need me, so I will let it slide this time." Brett glances at Grandpa Jake and he glances back at her as they walk through the door.

"Yes, we do," Brett says as they enter the cool interior. Natalie rushes inside and walks beside Brett.

"This is going to be fun."

* * * * *

They step out of the elevator into a brightly lit hallway. Paintings of pre-Columbian cities hang on the wall. Brett inspects them as they make their way down the tiled hallway. Their footsteps echo off the beige walls as they near the end of the hall.

They stop at a glass door with "History Department" written in black block letters across the top. The plaque next to the door details the names and office hours of the staff. Brett pushes open the door, and Natalie and Grandpa Jake follow her in. There is a large wooden desk in the center of the room and a petite lady with red hair and glasses looks up. "Good morning," she says. "Do you have an appointment?"

Brett walks up and stands in front of the desk. "Yes, ma'am," she replies. "We are here to see Dr. Hall." The lady looks at her over the top of her glasses as if inspecting something that is out of place.

"Brett Wilson?" she says.

"Yes, ma'am."

"Dr. Hall's office is down the hall, third door on the right."

"Thank you." Brett starts walking toward the hallway that leads off to the right of the reception area. The receptionist returns to her stack of papers and does not look up as Natalie and Grandpa Jake follow. Natalie counts the doors as she passes them. "One, two, three." She stops. "This is the one."

Brett takes a deep breath and knocks lightly on the wooden door. "Come in," says a muffled voice on the other side. Brett turns the knob slowly and pushes the door open. The office is small and cluttered with books and papers. The books on the desk are five high and in five or six stacks. Papers are in stacks of varying sizes on the corners of the desk. Behind the desk, Dr. Biven Hall is standing with her small, pale hand outstretched. Her light green eyes are bright and shining. "Good morning," she says in a slightly hoarse voice. "When Mr. Wilson called last night, I have to admit I was skeptical, but when he told me who he was I have to say my interest was piqued a little." She smiles broadly as she begins moving papers around on her desk. Her short blonde hair moves freely on her head as she makes different piles of the disorder. "I would have cleaned up, but I lost track of time."

"Thank you for meeting us on such short notice," Grandpa Jake says.

Brett looks over at him, still surprised that he trusted her information so much that he called for this meeting. "The pleasure is all mine," Dr. Hall says. "The story of Rock Wilson has become legendary here at Camden. People talk about nothing else. So, when you said you had some new information, how could I say no?"

Brett reaches into her cargo pants pocket and takes out her dark orange field book. She opens it to the map she has made and starts to speak. Dr. Hall waves her hand. "Where are my manners. Please take a seat," she says.

"I would rather stand," Brett responds.

Brett looks over at Natalie. Natalie's face is set firmly as she watches Dr. Hall. Brett can see that Natalie doesn't like the chaos of Dr. Hall's office, but she is doing an adequate job of hiding her displeasure. Grandpa Jake steps toward the desk and sits down in a folding chair. Brett places her field book on the only space on the desk.

"Have you ever heard of Gausili?" Brett asks rather quickly.

Brett eyes Dr. Hall, trying to read the expression on her face. Dr. Hall's bright green eyes become brighter as the seconds tick by. She begins rubbing her hands together in excitement. "A city visited by de Soto in 1540. There is still a certain amount of debate on where Gausili is and what de Soto was doing there." Brett glances over at

Natalie. Natalie appears to relax a little as Dr. Hall continues. "It is so far removed from the scope of exploration that de Soto was charged with."

"Do you know the location of Gausili?" Brett asks.

"There are differing beliefs on the current location of the city."

"Current location?"

"The Cherokee people believed that the Nunnehi lived in a city that changed locations."

"Nunnehi?" Brett and Natalie ask at the same time.

"Immortal spirit people who could make themselves visible when they wanted."

Dr. Hall eyes them with bright eyes that seem to dance. She is rubbing her hands together more vigorously as she talks. "It is very similar to the Zuni legend of a golden city that moves continuously"—a cold lump forms in Brett's chest—"the one Dr. Wilson investigated and ultimately found. That is extraordinary."

Natalie and Brett exchange a surprised look. Brett's mouth is dry as she tries to figure out what question to ask next—if there is any need to ask another question. "Where do you think Gausili is now?" Brett asks. She finds herself holding her breath as she waits for Dr. Hall to answer. Dr. Hall smiles broadly, showing her bright white teeth. "That is the million-dollar question," she says.

"No one knows for sure, but the legends say that the Nunnehi lived in underground townhouses in the Appalachian Mountains." Brett glances at Natalie.

"Do you believe it exists?" Natalie says.

"Just as real as Cibola," Dr. Hall replies. "De Soto went that far north for some reason. I bet he was looking for it."

"Did he find it?" Brett asks.

"That I don't know."

"Have any idea where we should start?" Natalie asks.

Dr. Hall smiles broadly and turns toward the bookcase behind her desk. She pulls two faded rolls of yellow parchment from the shelf and unrolls them on top of the desk. Papers flutter off the desk, catching the air current as they slowly fall to the floor. Brett steps closer to the cluttered table and stares down at an old map that appears to be drawn on an animal's skin. Natalie steps up next to Brett and reaches down to touch the parchment. "What's this?" she says.

Brett stares at the dark ink used on the parchment. The letters on the animal skin are rough and difficult to make out. She leans closer, and finally she notices, in the middle of the drawing, the name Gausili. It is a map, but it is different from the Hudson map that she has drawn in her field book. She takes the book and compares them. Gausili is shown to be further south than the location on her drawing. She looks up. "Is this map accurate?" she asks.

Dr. Hall grimaces. "Hard to tell. But I believe it could be."

"Have you ever checked it out?" Natalie says.

"You bet, but I never have heard a whisper from the Nunnehi," Dr. Hall says.

"A whisper?"

"The legends say that the Nunnehi would allow themselves to be heard, but when people looked for them, the sound would change locations."

"No one has ever seen them?" Natalie says.

"People have seen them, and even lived with them, becoming immortal."

Natalie looks at Brett as she traces the lines on the map. "Dr. Hall?" Brett says. "Would it be possible for us to borrow this?" Dr. Hall instinctively reaches for the parchment as if she is protecting it.

"Sorry," she says. "Can't let this out of my sight." Brett glances up at her.

"Can I make a copy?"

Dr. Hall's eyebrows shoot up quickly, and a slight smile forms on her face. "Let's make a bargain," she says sweetly. "How about I let you use my maps if you let me tag along."

Brett looks up at Dr. Hall without blinking. Dr. Hall smiles broadly as she picks up her maps and begins rolling them up. Brett is sure that she will need them—and the expertise of Dr. Hall—but she doesn't want someone that she doesn't know joining the expedition. She glances over at Natalie as she shifts her weight from the right to the left leg. Brett can tell Natalie is nervous for the same reasons she is, but she remains composed. She looks back at Grandpa Jake and he shrugs his shoulders.

Brett looks back at Dr. Hall. Her expression hasn't changed. She is still smiling, holding the rolled-up parchments tightly in her hands. "Alright," Brett says. "We get to use the maps. No strings attached."

Dr. Hall nods. "I want to find Gausili just as bad as you do, Ms. Wilson." The smile never leaves her face and her gaze never lowers.

"Deal," Brett says. She thrusts her field book back into her pocket. "Give us a few days to get all of our gear together."

"My mom will tell you when we start," Natalie says.

"Sure. Sure," says Dr. Hall. "Can't wait for the chance to study the areas around Newport."

"Newport?" Brett asks.

"The French Broad River near Newport, Tennessee," Dr. Hall says giddily. "That is the river de Soto sailed on."

Dr. Hall turns and places the drawing on the shelf behind her desk. "It is a pleasure joining your expedition, Ms. Wilson." Brett isn't sure how to respond, but she is a little uneasy about this new companion in their quest to find her dad.

"We will see you in a few days," Brett says. She turns and walks quickly toward the door. Natalie hurries after her. Brett can hear the loud footsteps of Grandpa Jake as she opens the door and steps out into the hallway.

CHAPTER 6

Arrow in Stone

It takes Brett four days to get all of her gear organized for the expedition to Newport. She stands in her room looking down at her desk. Maps of Newport are spread neatly across her desk. Brett takes a red pen and traces a line along the river. "Where did you go?" she asks as she looks down at the map. She picks up her journal and quickly scans the pages. She finds the diary entry of Luis de Moscoso, the leader of the group after de Soto's death. Moscoso is very descriptive concerning the topography and the location of different settlements further east from the great river. The descriptions correlate to the mountains found along a river in eastern Tennessee. Moscoso's information relates very well to the area around Newport.

Brett is also positive, based on Moscoso's account, that the great river is the Mississippi River. The fact that de Soto is buried in the river corresponds to the locations and descriptions given by Moscoso. Unfortunately, he never reveals the exact location of de Soto's final resting place.

Brett also has descriptions from Cherokee texts that she was able to find online. The more information she gathers from the native writings, the more it intrigues her. She finds that the correlations between the home of the Nunnehi and the city of Cibola have similar characteristics. She has the descriptions of Yahula, who is believed to have lived with the Nunnehi.

She also has six maps taped to pages inside the book. The first map is Charles Hudson's map, which shows the route of de Soto as he traveled through Florida, Georgia, South Carolina, North Carolina, and Tennessee. On the second page, there is an enlarged image of the Hudson map that shows specific areas in Tennessee and North Carolina. Gausili appears to be along a river in the northeastern portion of Tennessee.

The other maps are modern-day maps of the area. Brett picks up the book and pushes it into her favorite pair of brown cargo pants. She pulls her faded blue Royals cap down close to her eyes and grabs her backpack off the floor. She looks around the room, making sure that she hasn't forgotten some valuable piece of the de Soto puzzle. Satisfied, she throws her pack over her shoulder and walks out the door.

Outside the farmhouse, Dr. Brown is behind her Ford Escape, putting bags and a tent into the back. Natalie smiles as Brett walks down the steps. She rushes up to Brett, clapping her hands repeatedly. "This is so exciting," she says. Natalie sniffs the air. "Can you smell it? We are going to find the entrance. I just know it." Brett laughs as they walk toward the SUV.

"I like your confidence," she says.

Brett lays her bag in the overcrowded compartment in the back of the Escape and walks around to the rear door. Grandpa Jake is leaning against the SUV with his elbows resting on the hood. As Brett walks around the car towards the open back door, Grandpa Jake gives her a thumbs-up. She nods as she slides into the back seat. Natalie opens the door on the other side and peers inside. "Time to make history," she says. "We are going to be the only people to find two golden cities, and we've found them both in the last three months."

Brett rolls her eyes. "Get in the truck," she says. Natalie hops inside and bounces on the seat.

"We are so awesome!" she yells. Brett taps the journal that is secure in the pocket of her pants. With all the new information she has found, maybe this journey will be easier than finding Cibola. A smile spreads across her face as she thinks about all the information and the possibility of using the magnetoscope again. She should be able to find Gausili with the information she has found and the device Dr. Mies built.

Natalie continues bouncing on the seat next to her as Dr. Brown sits in the driver seat. She closes the door and turns to look at both girls. "No falling off a cliff this time," she says. Brett and Natalie nod in unison, then look at each other and smile.

"This is it," Natalie says. "Next stop Gausili." The smile on Brett's face grows larger as she watches her best friend.

"You know," Brett says, "I think we could be getting close to being awesome."

Natalie lets out a roar of laughter. "I've been waiting for you to say that for a long time." She continues bouncing as Dr. Brown puts the car in drive.

Brett watches as they roll by the fields where her goats are grazing in the distance. The smile doesn't leave her face as they turn right onto the main road. She is confident for the first time since watching Cibola disappear. She leans back in her seat and looks up at the bright blue sky. She is so close to finding her dad, and this time they are using the research that she has conducted. That is exciting. The white, billowing clouds roll through the blue abyss of the sky and Brett loses herself in the thought that this could all be over soon. The thought of success pushes away her apprehension about Biven Hall accompanying them. She will worry about her later. Right now, she is going to enjoy the ride and the feeling that she found the "X" on the map. That feeling gives her a sense of calm.

* * * * *

Brett watches the town of Newport, Tennessee appear as they travel northeast along Highway 411. It has been a three-hour drive from Camden, and Brett is ready to get out and explore the areas of the French Broad River that lie east of the city. She stares out the window at the shopping centers and commercial buildings as they drive through West End. In the rearview mirror she can see Dr. Brown's eyes darting from the road to the rear of the SUV.

The calmness Brett felt on the drive up begins to wane. *Why is Dr. Brown is acting this way?* She looks over at Natalie, who is sleeping soundly beside her. She turns and looks out the back glass of the Escape. A silver SUV is behind them, getting closer and closer. She can't take her eyes off the truck as it speeds toward them. The SUV pulls into the other lane and passes them. Brett turns and looks at Dr. Brown. "Can't be too careful," she says. Dr. Brown nods.

"After the last time. I'm not taking any chances."

A few months ago, Dr. Sims had them followed as he tried to steal her dad's field book. Dr. Sims is now in the city of Cibola, but he is working for a group called the Department of Antiquity Brett is sure that they are out there somewhere, waiting for her to find something that will help them. She sits back in her seat and watches the large ConAgra Foods building pass by on the left. They cross the Pigeon River and drive further out into the country.

The hills of eastern Tennessee fill the road ahead as they drive alongside the slow-moving French Broad River. The water looks like a pine-green ribbon that is around to tie a package on a present. The hills that stretch up from the water cast vibrant images on the pristine surface.

Brett tries to imagine what this river valley must have looked like when de Soto traveled down it in his flat-bottomed boats. The maps and descriptions she found seem to indicate that this is the waterway he used to explore southward into Tennessee. The French Broad empties into the Tennessee River, which flows south into Chattanooga and eventually into the Mississippi. That would be a direct water route from Newport to the great river.

This correlation excites her. De Soto was here, and she is here now, ready to unlock the mystery of Guasili. This is the place where he met with members of the Cherokee. Brett has a hunch that the information he gathered here led him to the second city of gold.

Dr. Brown turns right, and the vibrant white arches of the Wolf Creek Bridge stretch out across the river. Brett looks out the window as they pass over the tranquil stream. It doesn't look that deep from on top of the bridge. She can see the muddy riverbed rippling with the current of the water. They cross the short bridge, and a sign tells them the French Broad recreation area is down the narrow road to the right. Dr. Brown turns down the road, kicking gravel up as she turns too sharply.

Natalie finally wakes up from the sound of gravel hitting the wheel well of the SUV. "What did I miss?" she asks groggily, rubbing her eyes. Brett glances at her.

"The whole trip. We found Gausili and the map to the second city. We are heading home. Nothing left to find."

Natalie glares at her. "That's not cool," she says. Brett laughs.

"Of course it is."

"We are almost there," Dr. Brown says.

"What!" Grandpa Jake says shaking himself awake.

"Dr. Hall told us to meet her at the recreation center," Brett says.

Grandpa Jake rubs the stubble on his chin with his wrinkled right hand. "Be on the lookout," he says. Brett nods in agreement. The only people she trusts at this moment are the people sitting in the SUV.

"My thinking exactly."

"She acted weird when we met with her," Natalie says. She crosses her eyes and rubs her hands together as the tip of her tongue juts in and out of her mouth.

"Don't think she did that," Brett says. Natalie closes one eye and opens the other wide.

"She is super creepy and I'm going to keep this eye on her at all times," she says, pointing with a hooked finger toward her open wide eye.

"You do that," Brett says. Natalie continues flicking her tongue in and out of her mouth. Brett shakes her head and turns toward the window.

Dr. Brown pulls into the gravel parking lot of the recreation center. The building is rustic and looks like a log cabin from the eighteenth century, with big pine logs put together like Lincoln logs. Brett sits on the edge of the seat. She is so excited it feels like she is ready to burst. The hunt always did this to her when she was with her dad; now it is a little more intense since she is leading the expedition.

Brett takes her field book out of her cargo pants pocket and begins searching through the pages. This exercise always calms her. She quickly finds the maps she taped inside the book. She has studied the maps to the point where she can visualize locations on the maps without looking at them. She turns to the map she drew and uses her finger to trace the river they are parked next to. Brett thinks she has identified where de Soto started down toward the Tennessee River. She is certain that his jump-off point is the location of Gausili.

Dr. Brown parks beside a dark blue truck with a black camper top on the back. There is a "No Farms No Food" sticker on the back window of the camper, along with a sticker of what appears to be a thunderbird. Before Brett can get out, the doors on the truck open. Dr. Hall stretches her back and turns and waves at them. She isn't alone. There is a middle-aged man with red hair and glasses walking around the truck. He stands next to her with his arms folded across his chest and a sour look on his face.

Natalie moves over so she can get a better look. "He doesn't look happy to be here."

Grandpa Jake rubs the stubble on his chin. "Thought she was coming alone?"

Brett grips the book in her hands tight enough to make her fingers red. "Look at her. She's not going into the unknown without someone with her. We would bring someone we trusted," Brett says, not taking her eyes off the strange man.

Natalie slaps the seat. "Let's get going!"

Brett pulls her Royals hat down over her eyes and shoves the field book into her pocket. She opens the door and slides out of the car. The gravel crunches under her feet as her faded brown hiking boots touch the ground. She closes the door and walks toward a smiling Dr. Hall.

"Good day," Dr. Hall says joyfully. "It is a lovely place, don't you think?" She points to the surrounding hills to the right and left of the parking area. "You can only imagine what it must have looked like three hundred years ago."

Grandpa Jake, Natalie, and Dr. Brown walk over and stand next to Brett. Biven Hall turns her gaze to Natalie's mom. "Dr. Brown, this is an absolute pleasure. Your work is cutting edge, and I daresay I am a little overcome with fandom." Dr. Hall extends her hand. Dr. Brown looks down as if it might be a trick. She glances up at the smiling face of Biven and reluctantly shakes her hand. "This is great," Dr. Hall says. "Okay. Now for what we are here for."

Natalie cuts her eyes at Biven Hall and motions toward the man standing next to the doctor. "Who's this clown?" she asks as she glares at the red-haired man. "No offense, guy."

The man smirks as he stares back at Natalie. Dr. Hall glances over at the man and laughs. "Oh. This is Clarke Daly. He is an expert in colonial studies. Knows everything a person can know about the Spanish exploration of America." The smirk on his face seems to expand. Brett can see that his teeth are pressing tightly together. He seems to be impressed with his own importance and irritated at being in the presence of kids. He probably didn't like being called a clown or "guy." *Natalie is always adept at getting under someone's skin. She does have a gift.*

Biven Hall claps her hands together and motions for everyone to move toward the back of the truck. She grabs the latch to the camper top and pulls it open. Then she lays the tailgate down. There are rolls of paper in tubes inside the truck, along with shovels and other outdoor gear. She grabs a rolled piece of cracked and faded parchment, which she delicately lays on the surface of the truck and smooths flat. The parchment is made of coarse and wrinkled leather. Brett reaches out to touch it, but Dr. Hall instinctively brushes her hand away. "This is very old. So no touching," she says in an overly sweet voice. Dr. Hall takes a pair of white gloves and slips them on over her fingers. She pulls them tight and lays her hands on the parchment.

Brett leans down for a closer look. The blue ink on the leather has started to bleed in all directions from the original placement of the pen. It appears that the river has been drawn on the map, and various symbols are placed at different sections of the blue line. As she follows the lines, she can see some of the distinctive features of the area in which they are standing. The ridge in front of her in particular stands out on the map. She looks over at Natalie and Dr. Brown. They are staring at the map with supreme interest.

Biven Hall places her white-gloved hand on the map beside a bend in the river. "If I am correct, and I usually am, this is where we are standing." She looks up at the others, smiling.

"What do the symbols mean?" Dr. Brown asks as she points to the smooth, letter-like forms written in five locations along the large blue line. Biven Hall's eyes light up brightly.

"Thought you would never ask," she says. "These are the soundings that de Soto made along the river." Dr. Hall looks from Dr. Brown to Brett, waiting for them to see the significance. Brett knows that soundings are depth measurements taken at different locations in a channel. Why would de Soto take so many measurements along a small river?

Brett continues staring at the map, thinking about de Soto moving downstream and stopping at these points to take accurate readings and transcribe descriptions at each sounding point. "What are these other symbols?" Brett asks, glancing up into the smiling face of Biven Hall. "They don't fit with the others. The other symbols on the map are hand-drawn animals drawn in a blocky style." Brett notices what looks like a bear and an eagle. Beside each figure is a description, but Brett is unable to read it.

Clarke Daly steps forward and points to the map. "This one says, 'We have passed the Isle and ridden the shoe north and south.'" Brett takes in the new information. She will need to place this in her field book as soon as she can so she doesn't forget it. It sounds like a riddle that needs to be solved.

Clarke Daly looks up at them as he points to the next set of words. "'Follow the Chevron to the rippled hills; there the entrance will you find.'" Dr. Hall claps her hands.

"Gausili!" she screams. "Now, I'm sure you know just about where the entrance is since you came to me for the maps. Lead the way, Ms. Wilson, so we can make some history."

Brett looks down at the map. "Can I make a copy of this?" she says, pointing at the maps. "I would like a copy in my field book for reference later."

"Be very careful. These are quite old," Dr. Hall says. Brett quickly copies the markings on the piece of leather into the smooth pages of her field book.

She writes, "We have passed the Isle and ridden the shoe north and south," then writes the other clue neatly beside the thick blue line indicating the river. "Follow the Chevron to the rippled hills; there the entrance will you find." Brett places the pencil in her field book and studies the other two maps.

She is thinking about the clues and turns and walks toward the river. "She does this. Don't be alarmed," she hears Natalie say. Brett rubs her forehead with the back of her hand. The sun is rising higher in the sky, causing the temperature to change more rapidly. Sweat is forming on her brow as she struggles to decipher the clues written by de Soto. She walks back and forth, mumbling the words, "Ridden the shoe. How do you ride a shoe?" She flips from one page to another in her field book, trying to make sense of this new information. "Ridden past the Isle." That could be an island in the river. She searches her drawings, looking for an island that could have been in the river almost five hundred years ago, then she stops and looks intently at the maps again. It is highly unlikely that the Isle is still in the river considering the high rate of flow in the French

Broad during rain events. Brett moves her finger eastward, tracing the river, searching an area that would be ideal for an island formation. The exhaling air from her lungs catches in her throat as she finds a small bar of land jutting out into the channel of the river. It is roughly two miles from Wolf Creek Bridge. "If that is the Isle then the shoe should be to the west of the bridge." As she traces the river westward, her finger forms an inverted S curve. "Horseshoes," she says. There are two distinctive bends in the river—one pointing north and the other pointing south.

Her mouth is dry as she moves her finger further to the west. "Now I just need to find the Chevron and the rippled hills." She closes the book and heads back toward the other members of the party. They are silent as she walks up to the truck. "Time to go," Brett says. She opens the door and grabs her backpack and throws it over her shoulder.

"Let's do this!" Natalie yells as she grabs her bag and places it on her back.

The Chevron should be somewhere downstream of the shoe. Brett is sure of that. She leads the group out of the parking lot and across the narrow two-lane road. Her eyes move from left to right, scanning the different formations on the surface of the water. She studies the hill in front of her, which seems to grow from the edge of the river. "Which side of the river would the rippled hills be on?" she asks herself. She steps off the broken asphalt and down a grass-covered embankment. There are clumps of yellow-green and bright green grasses cascading down toward the sloshing water that laps at the bank.

There is almost perfect silence here along the French Broad River. She glances at the bluish-green water and can see the muddy bottom. She turns and walks west along the riverbank. The sun is high overhead, and the light reflects brightly off the surface of the slow-moving water. Brett's Royals cap isn't shielding her eyes as well as she would like. She squints, trying to shield her vision from the white, reflective light.

She moves through the low grass along the riverbank into taller and thicker grass. The long blades brush against the bare skin on her arms. It feels sharp as she moves through the waist-high greenery. Her mind continues replaying the riddle. *The Chevron to the rippled mountains.* A chevron is an inverted V-shaped mark on a badge or shield. De Soto used this to mark the location of something.

The river bubbles along to her right as she moves slowly along the grassy slope. "Finding a Chevron in this jungle of grasses is going to be difficult," she says out loud.

"You're not joking," Natalie says. "This stuff is thick."

"I kinda have an idea of where to look," Brett whispers.

"Of course you do."

Natalie turns and looks behind her. Dr. Brown is walking beside Biven Hall, and they look to be carrying on a hushed conversation. Clarke Daly is walking directly behind Biven, and his eyes are focused on Brett and Natalie. Grandpa Jake is twenty yards behind, walking slowly through the tall grass.

"I don't trust that guy," Brett says as they continue walking on the sloped bank of the river. "He creeps me out. He never blinks, and he is always staring at us." Up ahead the tall grass along the edge of the flowing water changes abruptly to a densely forested riverbank. The bright green leaves overhang the broad river, casting dark shadows on the light green surface. The thick rows of branches and leaves block out a lot of the sun's rays as Brett steps into the cool undergrowth.

She pushes her way through the branches of river birch, willow, and basswood. In some areas, she squeezes through small spaces between the intermingled branches. Brett and Natalie lose sight of Dr. Brown and Dr. Hall. Brett hasn't given the other companions much thought as she walks.

"What is the Chevron going to look like?" she says a little too loudly. Natalie glances at her.

"What?"

"The words on the map say that a Chevron will lead us to the rippled mountains," Brett says.

"Why is it when you're hunting treasure, the people that hid it are never specific? Why can't they say, 'Here it is?'"

"Where is the fun in that?" Brett asks.

"This is my second trip, and I just wish for once it could be easy."

"Have to work for the big reward," Brett responds.

"I suppose, but I don't have to like it."

They continue walking through the thick growth along the riverbank. The water gurgles and splashes near them as they climb over trunks of trees that reach out horizontally for the chance at touching the cool water of the river. Five minutes turns into ten, and still on they go, making slow progress. After thirty more minutes of walking, Brett takes out her field book and looks at her newly drawn map. She tries to see through the overhanging branches, but she can't see the other side of the river. She traces the river on the map. As far as she can tell, they are in the trough of the southern shore.

Brett reaches out and grabs a birch limb and pushes it upward. She can see the opposite side of the river now. She scans the riverbank, looking for a landmark she can use to accurately find their position. She looks east and west, studying the ridges that rise from the shoreline. The triangular peak to the northeast corresponds almost exactly to the south bend in the river. "Looks like we are getting close," Brett says as she returns the book to her pocket. "I just hope the Chevron is on this side of the river."

"With our luck, it will be on the other side," Natalie says, smiling.

"Have a little positivity," Brett says.

"Okay, I'm positive the Chevron thing is over there," Natalie says, pointing across the river.

Brett walks slower as they make the turn on the bank of the river. She searches along the ground for some sign that there is a marker present. "What do you think the Chevron is on?" Natalie asks. Brett focuses on the ground, looking for the sort of large stone that explorers used as markers. She examines the large boulders that litter the riverbank. Her heart begins to race as she runs her hands along the dark gray rocks. "You think it's one of these?" Natalie says. Brett nods as she drops to her knees so she can examine another large rock.

Natalie rushes ahead and starts looking at the surfaces of the rocks. Brett moves forward through the birch trees, investigating the layers of rock as she passes them. After twenty, then thirty, she starts to think that maybe she is on the wrong side of the river. It should be here, in this general area. Could her observations be wrong? What if the bends in the river aren't the shoes?

Brett takes a deep breath to calm her nerves. "This is it," she says.

Natalie looks up from a large rock. "Did you find it?"

Brett shakes her head and walks ahead to the next rock protruding from the ground. This isn't it. Brett turns as she hears twigs snapping behind her and sees Dr. Brown and Dr. Hall emerge out of the thick birch trees. Dr. Brown stops as she sees Brett and Natalie on the ground, running their hands on the surface of the rocks.

Dr. Hall claps her hands together loudly. Brett closes her eyes at the sound. She is growing tired of Dr. Hall's artificial excitement. "The Chevron?" she asks. Brett pretends not to hear her as she walks over to a rock that is abnormally square and sitting on top of a larger stone. It looks as if this rock has been placed by someone.

"Could this be the one?" She drops down until her face is inches from the coarse texture of the rock. She runs her hands along each side, trying to feel the indentations of a chevron. She feels each side once, then twice, but she feels only the round, sandy stone. The river could have weathered this large rock over the years. There is nothing there. No marks that were made by de Soto.

Brett slumps down with her back resting on the rock. Natalie continues searching, with no better results. Dr. Hall looks around at the large number of rocks littering the ground. "You searched all of them?" Brett nods. They have looked at every rock on this side of the river. "No markings at all?" Brett shakes her head, unable to speak. Clarke walks around a birch tree in front of her and eyes her suspiciously.

Brett gets to her feet and brushes the dirt from her pants. "Could be on the other side," she says.

Natalie looks out at the river. "Where we going to cross?" she asks. Brett walks toward the flowing green water. As she steps to the edge, she notices a large, square, blackish-gray rock laying on its side. She looks at the base and runs her fingers along the smooth surface. "This is a worked stone. Look at the flat surface. Not something you would find in nature. I bet this is the capstone. This sat on another stone, making a monument-like structure."

She looks closer and she can see a faint outline of what looks like a V. She takes out her field book and pulls her pencil from her pocket. She rips a piece of paper from the book and places it on the rock. "You found something," Dr. Hall says.

Brett focuses on the stone and begins rubbing her pencil across the paper. Instantly, a shield emerges on the page, along with an inverted V. Droplets fall from her saturated Royals hat. Dark splotches spread across the rubbing paper as her sweat soaks into the soft pages. She rubs the stone more vigorously and an arrow appears below the shield. The arrow points east, up the river in the direction they came. "The water, or something else, has knocked the stone off its platform," Brett says. She looks at Natalie. "Help me with this." As Natalie hurries over, Brett grabs one side of the stone; Natalie grabs the other, and the two girls struggle against the large rock.

It doesn't move.

Clarke Daly strides over confidently and helps them lift. The three of them lift the rock and place it on its pillar. "Thanks," Brett says. Clarke rubs his hands against the stone and follows the arrow toward the south. Brett gazes up the slope from the river, and her mouth falls open. She sees the ascending ripples of the ridge as clearly as if they were ripples on a pond. "There are the ripples," she says, pointing.

Clarke Daly looks up at the ridges sternly. "Indeed," he says.

"This is so exciting!" Dr. Hall exclaims. "Gausi-li is up there."

"A nice find, Doctor," Daly says.

"Everyone will know Dr. Biven Hall after I publish the paper showing that Gausili is real and has been found."

"Unimaginable wealth awaits," says Daly.

"Oh yes, of course," Dr. Hall says.

Brett glances at Natalie and motions with a nod her head toward Dr. Hall. Natalie nods slowly. Brett catches sight of Clarke Daly and sees a sneer spread across one side of his face. "Follow the arrow," Dr. Hall says as she ventures off up the slope, followed by Daly. Grandpa Jake almost falls as he steps through the branches of a weeping willow tree. Brett runs over to him and grabs his arm, trying to hold him up. "Think we found it Grandpa," she says. "But I think those two are going to try something." He stands up straight and steadies himself. "We can handle them," he says. "Don't worry about that." Brett holds onto his arm as they start up the slope toward the rippled ridge. *Whatever is here, it is ready to be found.*

CHAPTER 7

Mountain Oasis

The heat of the day presses on each of them as they move higher into the rippling ridges at the edge of the river. The air is thick with the evaporated water from the slow-current river below. It feels like a wet, heavy blanket hanging around Brett, constricting each breath. The air entering her lungs is hot and dense, making the journey up the slope more difficult. Brett can hear Natalie and Grandpa Jake's ragged breaths behind her.

Brett's blue Royals hat is two shades darker from the absorbed sweat that is soaking into the fabric from her brow. The saturated cloth can no longer hold another drop, and the sweat falls down her face and drops off her chin onto her damp shirt. Fallen pine and oak litter the ground, making the climb up the steep slope even more challenging. The boulders that have fallen down the slope create other obstacles that they must climb over or go around.

Dr. Hall and Clarke Daly are far up the slope ahead of them. They are both scampering over the harsh terrain with nimbleness and speed. The thrill of the hunt has clearly infected them as they push through the thick branches of fallen pines. Brett walks beside Grandpa Jake, continually reaching out to make sure he doesn't fall. "I'm alright," Jake says, out of breath.

"Sorry, Grandpa," Brett says.

Grandpa Jake stops and wipes his face with the back of his hand. "How much further do you think?" he asks.

"Not sure, Grandpa, but the rippled hills look like they go a few hundred more yards up the embankment," Brett says, staring up the steep slope. She points above the heads of Daly and Hall. "That is the second terrace we will come to," she says. "If this map is correct." She takes the field book out of her pocket and quickly turns to the map she has drawn. She points at the hills along the south side of the river. "That terrace is here," she says pointing. She looks up at Grandpa Jake. "Now, if I'm right, the flat area at the top of the slope is the location of the door" she says as she moves her finger up the first terrace to the second and stops on the third. The rippling hills are in a V-shaped pattern. It looks like a slice of pizza. The narrowest point is at the topmost terrace, extending outward, down the slope toward the river. It does indeed look like ripples on a lake, and Brett believes that where the ripples begin, that is where the entrance is located. *Just like when a stone is thrown into the water.*

The excitement starts building inside her. She can feel the blood pumping through her body as she looks down at the map. "We're almost there," Grandpa Jake says.

Brett looks up at him "Almost."

Natalie walks up beside her. "Why did you guys stop?" she asks. Brett closes the book and places it in the right side pocket of her cargo pants.

"Grandpa needed a little rest," Brett says, pointing at Grandpa Jake. "Kidding, Grandpa," she continues as he starts to protest. She looks at Natalie and points to the flat hilltop further up the rise. "The entrance is right up there."

"Why are we letting Happy Hall and Creepy Clarke get there before us?" Natalie furrows her brow and places her hands on her hips. "You don't think they will find it?" Brett shakes her head. Natalie laughs. The sound echoes all around them.

Brett looks up at the trees, her eyes darting from one to another. Not finding anything, she looks around at ground level. Natalie starts to say something, but Brett holds her index finger to her lips. Natalie closes her mouth. The forest is unusually silent. No birds are calling or flying. There aren't any calls from squirrels telling others where there are loads of acorns for harvest. There aren't any sounds of insects fluttering through the forest. Brett finds this to be particularly odd since they are close to a water source.

"What is it?" Natalie mouths.

"Listen."

They stand in silence for a minute until Natalie shakes her head. "I don't hear anything?" Dr. Brown stops and stands beside them.

"What is going on?" she asks. Natalie looks over at her, shaking her head.

"Waiting on you slowpoke," she says. "Now be quiet, we don't hear anything."

Brett looks into the motionless trees. "It is odd," she says. "There should be birds in the trees and mosquitos buzzing in our faces." Natalie looks at Brett with a questioning look.

"No mosquitos are a good thing, right?" Natalie says.

Dr. Brown stares at a thick oak tree that branches in three directions. "It is strange," she says. "There isn't any sound."

Brett rubs her chin with her sweat-drenched hand. "Yahula said that the forest lost sound before he saw the Nunnehi," she says.

"The nunne-who?" Natalie asks

"Immortal spirit people," Brett says. "Protectors of the Cherokee."

"Those are the people we are going to find?" Natalie asks, her voice shaking slightly.

"I believe they protect the entrance to the second city."

"You know you could let us know all this stuff before, so we aren't scared out of our minds," Natalie says.

"Where is the fun in that?" Brett says.

"We find the ghosts. We find the city," Natalie says calmly.

"And my dad."

Natalie looks up the slope. Dr. Hall and Clarke Daly are no longer visible. "Let's get moving," she says. She starts walking and climbs over a downed, rotting long-needle pine. Dr. Brown walks behind her. Brett looks at Grandpa Jake. He smiles at her and places his shaking hand on her shoulder. "You are an extraordinary girl," he says. "You are just like Rock. You know that." A smile spreads across her face. Her heart flutters in her chest at the thought of being compared to her dad. He is brilliant. He is a great explorer and a wonderful scientist. He is also the best dad.

"Thank you, Grandpa," Brett says.

"You have his intuition," Grandpa Jake says.

Brett takes a step up the leaf-strewn slope. Grandpa Jake continues talking. "Rock would be proud, and so would your mom." Brett stops. A chill pulses through her body at the mention of her mom.

"What?" she asks. Grandpa Jake hobbles toward her and places his hand on her shoulder.

"She would be extremely proud of your research and attention to detail. She was a well-respected expert on pre-Columbian American history."

She had never really thought about what her mom did for a living. She hadn't thought about the things she truly enjoyed. She had no idea that her mother was an expert in history. She stares out at the silent forest. The trees are still as she loses herself in the greens, browns, and grays of the sloping terrain. Maybe the note she found in her dad's desk was written by her mother. Maybe she was the source of information for her dad's expedition.

"Hey, Brett!" Natalie yells from far up the tree-covered rise. Brett blinks three times as she tries to focus on where the voice is coming from, until she sees Natalie waving through the dense green foliage. "Get moving, will you? I can't even see where they have gone." Brett focuses her eyes on the angled ground ahead of her, but she listens for any sound coming from the forest. She will have to wait to think about whether her mom is the one giving her clues through her writings. Now she has to focus all her attention on the task at hand. She will locate whatever is up there, hidden in the shade of the trees. Once that task is complete, she will search for answers to the questions she has about her mom.

She slows down to match Grandpa Jake's pace as he hobbles along beside her. She has her arms ready just in case she needs to catch him. Brett scans the dark expanse of the forest as they walk up the slope. Their footfalls do not create a sound, despite stepping through brittle fallen leaves.

At last Brett and Grandpa Jake top the rise. The ground flattens out for another fifty yards before it returns to the steeply angled ascension to the top of the ridge. Brett is breathing hard as she walks across the flat ground toward Natalie and Dr. Brown. Natalie is standing with her foot up on a log, tapping impatiently. "About time," she says. "Thought we would have to find it without you this time."

Brett and Grandpa Jake stop next to Natalie and look up the tree-lined ridge. "You could have," Brett says with a smile. Natalie shakes her head.

"We would have gotten lost and that would have been something else you would need to find," Natalie replies. "I did think about it though."

Brett searches through the thick oak trees for movement. "I know you did," she says as she takes off her blue Royals hat and wipes her brow with her shirt. The forest appears darker as the sun overhead passes behind a large white cumulus cloud. The hot, humid air grows a little cooler without the heating rays of the sun.

"I don't think we're going to beat Dr. Hall and Daly," Natalie says.

"No need to worry about that," says Brett. Dr. Brown searches Brett's face.

"You think something is going to happen?" Dr. Brown asks.

"It is a possibility," Brett says placing her hat back on her head.

"That's just great," Natalie says. "And look. The scary, silent forest has gotten a bit darker. And you know that something creepy is just lurking out there in the shadows waiting for us to pass by."

Brett pulls her hat further down over her eyes. "Let's go," she says. Brett and Grandpa Jake step around a large white oak, avoiding the hanging branches. Brett can hear Natalie talking behind her.

"You guys go first," Natalie says. "Safer that way." She looks at her mom. "At least there isn't a hundred foot drop off this time."

Brett and Grandpa Jake pass deeper and deeper into the darkness of the forest. The thick canopy of trees does an effective job of out keeping any rays of sunlight. Up ahead, two large boulders stand like sentinels among the trees. Thick privet bushes have grown up along each side of the gray rocks. Between the rocks is a narrow pathway that has been cut by flowing water making its way from the top of the hill down to the river below. Brett and Grandpa Jake stop. Brett runs her fingers along the rock, feeling the smooth undulations of the wet surface. Water has passed over the rock repeatedly, creating soft ripples on the surface.

"We need to go through that dark and scary path, don't we?" Natalie asks as she walks up behind them. Brett nods her head and looks intently at the tops of the boulders. The vertical stone columns are tall and cast dark shadows over the narrow stone pathway that leads upward. The alley through the rocks is eerily dark. "Maybe we can wait for a bit of sunlight to light up the path," Natalie says as she looks up at the sky, now blanketed by dark clouds. "That's not going to work," she sighs. "Thank you, clouds."

Brett steps onto the first stone that leads forward onto the gloomy path. It is perfectly smooth. Brett studies the rock. She knows that in nature rock rarely forms smooth right angles. "Someone made this stairway." Brett says. "Great." Natalie says behind her. Brett leans down and looks closely at the steps that lead higher. "Almost perfect." She turns and looks at Natalie. Natalie grimaces. "I'm following you," she says. Brett turns and looks up the stone stairway toward the summit. This is a fantastic discovery. A pathway carved out of stone with an entrance at the top. It reminds her of the Incan roadways carved through the Andes Mountains in South America. There are about forty rock steps until they reach the top. "We have to be getting close," Brett says as she starts up the slippery path. Water drips off the high rock walls and falls onto the gray stone. Even the water striking the stone is silent in this part of the forest. Brett keeps her eyes focused on the treacherous path ahead as she climbs over waist-high stones that have fallen from the summit.

As they near the top of the stone steps, a soft breeze blows from the bottom of the gap in the rocks to where she is standing. The moving air feels cold on her sweat-soaked skin. When Brett is six steps from the top the air moving around her increases in speed, blowing her blonde hair out from under her Royals hat. She takes another step and stops abruptly. The hair on the back of her neck is standing straight up. Brett hears a faint whisper in the swift breeze. She can't make out what the voice is saying.

"What was that?" Natalie asks.

Natalie grabs the back of Brett's shirt and pulls. "Tell me you heard that." Brett strains her ears to make out what the whispering voice is saying.

"We know why you have come."

The words emanate from the air flowing around them. Brett turns and looks at Natalie. Natalie is pale and looks ready to fall down the stone stairway, if not for her tight grip on Brett's shirt. "Not good when the air starts talking to you," Natalie says, her voice shaking.

Dr. Brown looks at Natalie and Brett with her mouth slightly open. Grandpa Jake closes his eyes as the voice continues, more audible this time. "We know what you seek." The voice seems to come from all around them as if they are surrounded, but it isn't harsh. Brett feels a sense of calm as she hears the voice on the wind. She turns and looks up toward the top of the slope.

"Are you the Nunnehi?" she asks calmly. A soft breeze blows down from the top of the stone pillars, and as the wind passes, a male figure with long dark hair and dark eyes emerges from the rock face in front of her. Natalie lets out a gasp.

The man is wearing a light brown tunic that falls to his upper thigh and what looks like a pair of loose-fitting leather pants. He takes one step toward them. "You seek Gausili," he says with a soft, rhythmic voice. Behind her, Brett can hear other voices agreeing with the man.

"Yes," she responds with a gravelly voice caused by the dryness of her mouth. The man sits on one of the stones steps and studies the group intently.

"Why do you search for a place that has remained hidden from your world?"

Behind them, other voices echo the question. "Why."

Brett glances back at Grandpa Jake, Dr. Brown, and Natalie. She can see the fear radiating out from their strained faces. She turns back to the man. He picks up a gray stone from the ground and rolls it through agile fingers. His eyes remain fixed on her. She licks her lips and moves her hat back so that her eyes can be seen. "We need to find Gausili so that I can find my dad." Brett says slowly.

The man cocks his head to the left and narrows his eyes. "How will finding this sacred place help locate your father?"

"He entered Cibola and the city disappeared, and I believe that this place is the entrance to a city like it," Brett says. The man places the stone on top of a larger rock. He then picks up a smaller stone and places it gingerly on top of the others. He stacks six stones on top of the larger stone, and he never takes his eyes off her. Brett studies the small rock tower. She isn't quite sure what he is doing.

"Cibola you say," the man says. He points to the stone directly in the middle. "Gausili," he says, pointing at the small stone on top. "This is what you believe will happen if you find it." He runs his finger from the top down to the rock representing Cibola. "You can travel from one point to another." He studies her face intently as he says the words. Brett licks her lips again.

"That is what I believe," she says.

He takes a step back from the rock towers and looks around as if he is searching for something. A whisper starts from where the man is standing but his mouth doesn't move. Brett tries to understand what is being said, but the sound is too low. "Very well," he says. "You will come with us."

Brett stares at the man. "What do you mean?"

"You will come with us, now," he says forcefully.

"Why?" Brett and Natalie say together.

"You are in danger," he says as he turns toward the gray stone pillar.

"How?" Brett says, feeling the coolness around her body.

"Bad men are coming for you."

He motions for them to follow him. He stands facing the large gray boulder and waits for them to join him. Brett looks at Natalie. Natalie shrugs her shoulders and looks back at Dr. Brown. "We must be quick," the man says. "They are almost here." Brett does not like the idea of being hunted. Who was it this time? Other questions pop into her brain, and her mind races trying to answer a few of them.

"Let's go," she says to the others. As they step behind the man, a bright light instantaneously appears on the surface of the boulder. The man casually walks into the light and disappears.

Brett takes a deep breath and steps into the shining bright rock. In an instant, she is transported from the rocky stairway into a large circular room. There are wooden seats positioned around the outside wall of the room. The floor is made of dirt, and it is as smooth as glass. Other dark-skinned men and women are watching her. She looks behind her as Natalie, Dr. Brown, and Grandpa Jake materialize out of the air. "Where are we?" Natalie says breathlessly.

"A townhouse of the Nunnehi," Brett says.

CHAPTER 8

Cherokee Trail

The large, circular room is neither hot nor cold. It is the perfect temperature for a hot summer day. The indigenous people watching her remain motionless as Brett scans the perimeter of the room. When they breathe, their chests do not rise or fall. They don't blink their eyes as they stare at her. The man that led them through the shining doorway in the rock steps forward. "It is uncommon for us to have visitors like you," he says, waving his hand through the air.

Brett watches the man move his hands in perfect unison, forming small circles and large looping circles in the air. His black hair frames his square chin perfectly. His dark eyes remain focused on her as he continues moving his hands through the air. Brett can hear the faint whispers

filling the air around her, but the sounds are inde-
cipherable. After a few minutes, he continues in
a melodic voice, "You have come seeking the entrance to Gausili." The words hang in the air and
his voice seems to echo all around her.

Brett can't speak. It is like she is hypnotized by
the motion of the man's hands and the peaceful
sound of his voice. "To find your father," he says.
"Such a perilous journey for someone so young."
The whispers around her flow at a faster rate, as
if the speakers are speaking hurriedly. Brett looks
away from his choreographed motions and catches sight of Natalie and Dr. Brown. They are standing a few yards away from her, staring straight
ahead. They appear to be in a trance-like state.
Brett gets the impression that they are sleeping
standing up. Grandpa Jake appears the same way.

Brett looks back at the man. His eyes narrow.
"I do not think that you are ready for this journey," he says. Hearing those words, Brett is finally
able to muster her courage and force herself to
respond.

"I am ready, and I will find him." She holds her
head high. "I figured out how to find Cibola, and
I figured out how to find Gausili. And I will bring
him home."

His narrowed eyes seem to penetrate into her
very soul. She can feel the heat building inside
her. She isn't sure if it is her anger building or

the searching eyes of the native man before her. The man kneels and begins drawing circles in the smooth dirt. He keeps his eyes on her. "Did you not have assistance?" he asks. "From your elders?" These words cut at her self-confidence as they reverberate in the air around her: "From your elders. From your elders." He shakes his head. "These people helped you, yes?" She places her hands over her ears, trying to keep the sound out of her head, but the man's voice continues as loudly as before.

The man lowers his eyes and shakes his head. "You are not ready for what lies ahead." Brett grits her teeth and takes her hands off her ears.

"I am!" she says. She glares at him as he continues drawing circular patterns in the dirt. "I know I had help. I know that my dad, Dr. Brown, Grandpa, and Natalie have helped. It hasn't been just me." The words spill out of her mouth like water flowing from an artesian spring. "I would not be here without them, and I would not be here without you."

His hands stop moving and his fingers remain on the dirt circle he has just drawn. He looks up at her slowly, and a slight smile crosses his face. "Maybe I was mistaken. Maybe someone so young can lead this expedition and find the link between worlds." Brett can't fully comprehend what he has just said. Her mind fumbles over his words as she tries to piece the information together.

The link between worlds. She can't take her eyes off of his face, and his smile grows a little larger. It is like he can hear the conversation she is having inside her head. He remains silent, giving her time to bring herself to a conclusion.

"I can get there from here?" she says.

"Not from here."

"Gausili."

"Yes."

"Can you help me find it?"

The man stands up as the smile vanishes from his face. He steps closer to her and holds out his smooth, thick hand. "We will help you as we have already. We protected you from the trackers, and now we will guide you on the next leg of your odyssey." Brett looks down at his hand. His palm is facing her, and she can see the lines running along it. She hadn't noticed how muscular he is until now. He has a physical strength that gives him the appearance of a great warrior.

"Thank you," she says. With his outstretched hand he motions for her to follow him.

Brett looks at Natalie, Dr. Brown, and Grandpa Jake as the man starts to walk away. "What about them?" The man doesn't stop walking. He waves his arms in a broad, looping circle, and instantly

Natalie, Dr. Brown, and Grandpa Jake begin blinking their eyes.

"Now, follow me," he says. "There is much that we must discuss." He walks across the smooth dirt surface toward the series of benches that line the outside wall of the circular building. Brett follows him, ready for the unknowns ahead.

* * * * *

The man watches them as he sits down on the long, smooth, oak bench. Brett looks at Natalie and shrugs her shoulders. She sits down, a row below the man. He observes them intently as they sit below him. "I am Atohi," he says. "We have lived in these mountains for thousands of years. We have protected wayward travelers, and we have protected our people." His eyes are bright as he talks. "And we have protected the entrance to Gausili." His dark black eyes move from Grandpa Jake to Brett. "The entrance is in danger once again." Brett's stomach flutters uncontrollably.

She takes off her Royals hat and holds it in her hands. She hopes that Atohi doesn't see that her hands are shaking slightly. "Mr. Atohi, why is the city in danger?" she asks.

He closes his eyes slowly and rubs his forehead with his long fingers. "You do not know?" Brett glances over at the others. This time Natalie shrugs her shoulders. "Maybe we misjudged you," he says.

Brett shakes her head. "You haven't made a mistake, but I don't fully understand what is going on," she says with her voice rising.

"You know we are the Nunnehi, correct."

"Yes."

"You know what we are? Yes."

"Spirit people of the Cherokee," she says confidently.

"You know our task?"

"Yes."

He places his arms upon his knees and looks at her. She feels the physical energy being transmitted from his eyes into hers. The pulse of energy radiates through her head into the very core of her mind. He is searching her in a pointed examination. *How is he doing this?* He lifts his chin and flexes his fingers. "I do believe we have chosen correctly," he says. She feels light-headed as the energy flows out of her mind and down her neck and dissipates in her body. She shakes her head, trying to get rid of the fuzziness in her brain. "The Nunnehi are here to help you on your journey, and you will do what you have been called to do," he says.

The buzzing in her mind slowly dissipates, allowing her to focus on what Atohi is saying. Questions start popping into her mind as she processes his words. "You will help me find Gausili?" A small smile spreads across his face and he nods his head slowly. "And you said that we could not find it from here." Again, he nods. "But you will guide me?" He nods. Her mouth is dry, and she feels confidence building inside her. She is sure of what she must do. "To find Gausili, I need something else?" she says. She opens her backpack and pulls out the magnetoscope and shows it he Atohi.

Atohi studies the square metal device without touching it. "I can use something like this, can't I?" Brett asks. He doesn't take his eyes off the magnetoscope.

"The way to Gausili is shrouded in the folds of space, and this helps locate objects in space," he says. "Unfortunately, Gausili is also hidden by the fluctuations of time." Brett glances at Dr. Brown to see if she understands what Atohi is saying. "Places, people, and things all occupy space in our world, but they also occupy that space at a particular time."

Brett struggles with this new information. *How can it be shrouded?* She remembers the shimmering city of Cibola materializing out of nothingness. She had used the mangetoscope to find the space, and Dr. Brown had figured out when the magnetic anomaly would present itself. "Each of these cities will become visible to our space and time at different intervals. So, to find Gausili, I need the exact time that it will become visible," Brett says.

Atohi claps his hands together. It is the first time he has shown any degree of excitement. "Yes," he replies. "We have supplied this information to travelers before." Brett looks to her right. Grandpa Jake and Natalie are staring at her, bewildered by the conversation.

"How?" she says. "How do you know the time?" Ahohi slowly stands. He towers over her, but he is not scary. His broad smile seems to grow larger. "There is a way," he says, drawing the cross in the air. "With this."

"A cross shape?" Brett asks.

"This will help locate the place and time," Atohi says. "We gave it to the last one who searched for the city. It is made of the finest metal from the mountain and is inlaid with blue quartz. It is the perfect tool to find Gausili."

"Gausili moves just like Cibola."

"We are all moving through space and time."

"Who did you give it to?" she asks.

"You know this already."

"De Soto."

He solemnly shakes his head. "Beware. Others are searching for the object, so you must be very careful." *The trackers are still hunting for Gausili.* They are still hunting for this cross—and they are still hunting her. "I see you are troubled," Atohi says. "Be of good courage. You have loyal companions. They will help you." Brett looks at Natalie. Natalie gives her a thumbs up.

Atohi motions for the others to stand. Dr. Brown, Natalie, and Grandpa Jake stand up beside Brett. She is grateful to have all of them with her. She would not want to venture into the unknown with anyone other than them. "The Nunnehi will protect you on your journey down the mountain, but our power will not venture beyond that." Atohi says.

"I would like to thank you for all that you have done," Brett says. Atohi puts his hands together and lowers his head.

"Now we must go," he says softly.

He steps down the wooden planks of the benches and strides toward the center of the round structure. Brett and the others follow close behind. Brett thinks about where she must go next. She remembers the map she drew earlier in the day—the map Dr. Hall had allowed her to see. She doesn't have access to the original any longer, but her copy is almost a perfect rendition. She thinks about where de Soto went after he left the area around Newport. From the maps, it appears that he continued down the French Broad River. He then floated down the Tennessee River until he reached Tennessee's border with Georgia.

Brett follows Atohi out of the circular structure. She studies the cone-shaped building and marvels at its enormous size. This building could hold hundreds of people. "Our time together is almost over," Atohi says without looking back at her. "You will emerge from our village at the base of the slope." He walks onward over the smooth, grassy surface. It is like a cushioned carpet beneath Brett's feet as she follows. Finally, Atohi stops in front of a tall, square, gray-and-white rock with circular carvings around the edges. He turns to the group and begins drawing a circle in the air.

"You must move quickly," he says. "Our protections will only last for a short period."

Brett stops beside him. "Thank you again for everything," she says. He smiles and places his strong hands on her shoulders.

"We have chosen wisely," he says. He looks up at the stone pillar. A light begins pulsing on the sides, causing the boulder to shift from gray to a titanium-white color. "Be on your guard and follow the path of the ancient people. Their spirit will guide you to the cross." The stone glows bright white.

"Thank you," Brett says, and she steps into the bright glow of the rock. The air is squeezed out of her and instantly she is standing on the leaf-strewn ground at the base of the rippled hills.

Brett turns and watches a large boulder that looks like it has fallen from the top of the slope as it pulses in vibrant light. Natalie steps out of the doorway and nearly falls to the ground. Brett grabs her and keeps her upright. "That was graceful." Natalie says. The white light flashes again, and this time Grandpa Jake gingerly steps through the doorway. Another pulse and Dr. Brown is standing with them. The light around the large rock disappears, leaving the dull gray boulder towering over them.

"Let's get going," Brett says. "We don't want the trackers to find us."

"We don't want Dr. Hall and Daly finding us either," Natalie says.

Brett looks at Grandpa Jake to make sure he is ready for the return trek. She reaches out to grab his arms, but he shakes his head. "Atohi said we needed to hurry. I can make it," he says. Brett nods, then walks quickly out toward the riverbank before turning her back on the setting sun and hurrying eastward. They should make it back to the SUV before it gets dark. She turns and looks behind her. Grandpa Jake is shuffling along, walking as fast as she has ever seen him. Natalie steps over the downed logs behind Grandpa Jake, with Dr. Brown in the back of their formation.

Brett scans the thick undergrowth as she moves through the dense thicket along the French Broad

River. The sound has returned. Birds chirp happily in the trees overhead and the river gurgles as it flows over the smooth rocks on the bank. Brett listens intently, trying to filter through the natural sounds so she can pick up any sounds of pursuit. She can hear the crunching of leaves behind her as Grandpa Jake and Natalie try to keep up with her pace.

They make good time as they crash through the thick forest surrounding the river. They pass by the two bends in the river, and Brett can see the center where they parked up ahead. A smile spreads across her face as she steps into the clearing. They made it, and it seemed to take a much shorter time on the return journey.

Natalie runs up beside her as she walks up the slope toward the SUV. "Where are we headed to now, boss?" Natalie says. Brett looks over at Natalie with narrowed eyes.

"Boss. Really."

"You are the boss," Natalie says. "So, where we headed this time?

"Follow the map to the final resting place of the cross."

They walk into the gravel parking lot. Their feet crunch on the crushed limestone gravels with each step. "You know where it is, don't you?" Natalie says.

Brett shakes her head. "I have an idea." They walk three more steps before Dr. Brown calls out behind them.

"They are here!"

Brett turns and sees Dr. Brown and Grandpa Jake running toward them. Grandpa Jake is hobbling more than running. Behind them, four men are sprinting out of the thicket along the river, through the clearing and toward the slope to the parking lot. Brett grabs Natalie and they run as fast as they can toward the white SUV.

Brett's baseball hat nearly flies off her head as they sprint toward the Ford Escape. The lights on the rear of the car flash. Dr. Brown must have unlocked the doors with the remote. Brett turns to look behind them as she races forward over the crunching gravel. She can see the head and torso of the first man as he makes it to the level parking lot. He has a smooth face that comes to a distinctive point at his chin. His dark hair is cut short, and he runs with ease. The three other men come bounding into view behind him. They are wearing dark-colored pants and white shirts, and each of them looks extremely angry.

Brett and Natalie hurry to the SUV and throw the back doors open. Brett grabs the handle to the front door and opens it. Dr. Brown won't have to open it; she can get in and they can make their escape. Natalie, seeing Brett open the front door, climbs over the seat and opens the door for Grandpa Jake. Brett slides into the back seat and watches out the window. The men are gaining on Dr. Brown and Grandpa Jake. Twenty feet, ten feet. Finally, Grandpa Jake rounds the back of the Escape and throws himself into the seat.

Dr. Brown has the key in the ignition before she sits down. The SUV roars to life. Brett can't take her eyes off their pursuers. She can see their mouths moving as they talk to each other. They are almost to the SUV when Dr. Brown slams it into reverse and accelerates toward the charging men. The first two scamper out of the way as the SUV speeds toward them. Dr. Brown stops, shoves the shifter into drive, and slams her foot down on the gas pedal. The tires spin in the gravel and can't get traction to move forward. Brett watches in horror as the man with the pointy chin runs over to the Escape in a flash and wrenches open Dr. Brown's door.

Brett can see the fear emanating from Dr. Brown's face as the man grabs her left arm. "Let go of her!" Natalie yells as Brett tries to climb toward the front seat. Natalie is also starting to climb through the gap between the two front seats. They have the same plan: try to hit, scratch, or bite any part of their attackers so that they can get away.

Dr. Brown keeps her foot on the gas and the tires spin through the loose gravel. Clouds of dust envelop the SUV from the friction between the tires and the surrounding rock. Brett is finally able to grab the wrist on the man with the pointy chin. His eyes dart to her, and a sneer spreads across his smooth face. Brett is clawing at his flesh to get him to release Dr. Brown, but he laughs.

The passenger door flies open and another man stands in the doorway. Grandpa Jake swings his fist wildly and hits him in the stomach. The man doubles over in pain, and Grandpa Jake swings again, this time connecting with the man's face. He falls backward as Grandpa Jake grabs the door and closes it.

The SUV lurches forward as the smoking tires grab the solid ground beneath the gravel. The rear of the Escape begins spinning to the right, pulling the man toward the inside of the car. Dr. Brown screams as he grips her tighter. Brett digs her fingernails into his wrist. The man stumbles forward as the Escape grabs the firmness of the ground and quickly speeds toward the asphalt road ahead. He releases Dr. Brown and wrenches his wrist away from Brett. He throws himself out of the SUV, bouncing off the gravel into the lush green grass.

Dr. Brown grabs the door and closes it as the Escape nears the black surface of the road. Brett turns and looks out the back window. Three of the men are chasing them on foot, but where is the fourth? Suddenly there is a crash on top of the SUV. Brett can see a pair of legs dangling down over the windshield. "He's on the roof!" Natalie yells. Dr. Brown presses the gas and gravel flies up behind them. They race out onto the asphalt highway, and as Dr. Brown turns sharply to the right the man falls from the top of the car. Brett watches as the man slams into the ground and rolls into the grass. He pops up quickly and stares after them.

"Is everyone okay?" Dr. Brown asks, her voice shaking.

Brett's heart is racing as she sits back in her seat. She looks over at Natalie. Natalie shakes her head as she buckles her seat belt. "Every time. Every time," she says. "It would be nice if just once we could try to find something without fearing for our lives." She looks out the window with wide eyes.

Dr. Brown accelerates the SUV quickly down the narrow, two-laned road. The trees whip by in a blur as Brett looks out the window at the pale green water of the slow-moving French Broad River. She turns and looks out the back glass, expecting the trackers to be right behind them. But the roadway is empty, and Dr. Brown continues to increase their speed as they round the turns that pass along the edge of the river. The white columns of Wolf Creek Bridge spring into view as Dr. Brown glides around a curve in the road, all the while continuing to search the rearview mirror for any pursuers.

She slows down slightly as they near the intersection that will take them across the river. As the SUV hits the main road, Dr. Brown accelerates quickly. They cross the bridge in seconds and turn left onto Highway 70. They need to get as far away from the trackers as possible. Brett looks out the window at the tranquil water. Thoughts of the day come flooding into her mind. She has experienced some extraordinary events in just a few hours. She met a member of the Nunnehi. The thought of visiting their village lifts her spirits a little. They protected her just as they had protected the Cherokee people. That is a humbling thought.

Atohi also gave her the direction that will take her onto the next leg of the journey. She reaches into her side pocket and takes out her field book. The cover is starting to fray on the spine; it is starting to look like her dad's own book. She looks at it absently, thinking about her dad. He is out there, wanting to get back here. Brett opens the book carefully and slowly turns the pages to the maps.

Natalie looks at her, biting her lip. "Do you think those guys will beat us to where we are going?" she asks.

Brett glances up at her. "I bet there are more of them out there than just those four."

Natalie puts her head back on the headrest and closes her eyes. "I thought you would say that."

Brett looks down at the Charles Hudson map that she has taped in her book. She traces the thick red line of de Soto's route from Newport to the place where he entered Georgia. She compares it to her copy of Dr. Hall's map. Both maps indicate the same route, and Brett places her finger on the exact spot on the drawing. "It looks like Chattanooga is our next stop," she says without looking up from the map.

She is certain that the next clue will be found there, but she isn't sure where it will be found. The answer is in the drawing that Dr. Hall let her use. That drawing helped her locate the rippled ridges, and now she is going to use it to find de Soto's cross. "You did good back there, kid." Grandpa Jake says. Brett looks up at him. His face is weathered and tired, but his eyes sparkle brightly as he looks at her.

"Thanks," she says with a smile. Grandpa Jake settles into his seat and starts rubbing his left knee. He is probably in a lot of pain. Brett feels responsible for the danger she has brought to her family and friends.

She looks up and notices Dr. Brown staring at her through the mirror. *How long has she been watching me?* Brett lifts the sweat-stained hat off her head and places it on her knee. Dr. Brown seems a little uncomfortable as she continues staring at Brett. "Chattanooga?" she finally says. Brett nods. Dr. Brown returns her eyes to the road. "We will be there in about three hours." Those three hours will seem like an eternity to Brett, but they will give her time to figure out where she will need to look. The cross could be there, and she will probably need all three hours to find the spot.

Dr. Brown drives the SUV just above the speed limit through Newport. After a few minutes, they pull onto Interstate 40 and head west. They are chasing the sun that is slowly migrating across the pale blue sky. Brett thinks about how de Soto must have traveled along a similar path, gazing at this same sky. The vast expanse of blue holding the hope of discovery. Brett sits back in her seat and gazes down at her book. She will find the cross. She will find her dad.

CHAPTER 9

The Bend

The fading rays of sunlight filter out over the ridges to the west of Chattanooga as Dr. Brown drives south along Interstate 75. Bright yellows and oranges illuminate the dark blue sky, sending radiant light to every corner of the ridges and valleys of the landscape. Brett glances up from her book as they pass under a large green sign that stretches across the road. "Chattanooga 10 miles."

Brett stares up at the sky. Thin, wispy clouds migrate from west to east in a slow-moving current. Brett returns her gaze to the map in her book. There on the map are descriptions of where de Soto stopped along his path through Tennessee. He left Newport and traveled southward on the Tennessee River, maintaining close contact with the river for its readily available food and water. The river also provided a faster mode of transport for themselves and their supplies.

The de Soto expedition stopped many times along the way, but the one place that is mentioned with a complete description is a well-developed river village between the ridges. The central structure of the village was a large, circular building made of wood with a roof of dried, bundled grass. Around this, there were rectangular buildings made of wood. De Soto describes staying in one of the rectangular buildings for almost a month in 1540.

He describes the village as being along the east side of the river at the flat-topped mountain. De Soto set anchor and came ashore there, bringing trinkets of blue and red glass chevron beads as gifts for the people of the river valley.

Brett studies the map again and again as they travel along the interstate. She is certain that the flat-topped mountain is Lookout Mountain. She scans the topographic map for a promising spot where the city might be found—"along the river plain between the two ridges," according to de Soto's description.

She takes a pencil from her book and traces the line indicating the river. She stops at the base of Lookout Mountain. There is a distinctive bend in the river at the foot of the mountain, across the river from a flat plain that lies on a north-south trajectory. She lightly draws an X at the tip of the valley, where the apex of the bend in the river is most pronounced.

Natalie looks over at the drawing. "That's where we are headed?" she asks. Brett moves her pencil north across the map to the base of the ridge to the west. It fits. The city should be between those two points.

"I think so," she responds in a confident tone. Brett looks up at Natalie. Natalie doesn't take her eyes off the map.

"You think those men will be there?"

Brett shrugs her shoulders. "Probably. They have the originals. So, yeah. I think they will be there."

"That's just great."

"I'm hoping we can get in and get out before they show up."

"Not likely though, right?"

Brett shrugs again. Natalie shakes her head. "You could say something that is reassuring. Like, 'Of course, we will find the cross thing before those trackers get there. No danger this time.'" Natalie throws her head back against the seat. "I know. I know. No danger no reward."

Brett sits up in her seat and holds the book out so Dr. Brown can see it through the rearview mirror. "Dr. Brown," she says, "I think I've found where we need to go."

Dr. Brown shakes her head. "Where?"

Brett clears her throat. Her mouth is chalky and dry. "Moccasin Bend, judging by the descriptions and the map." She swallows hard. Brett can see the worry etched in Dr. Brown's face. Brett doesn't like leading them into danger, and it seems like every time they are on an expedition now, trouble finds them.

"Okay. We just need to be careful. And we need to stay alert." Dr. Brown grips the steering wheel tightly and steers through the late afternoon traffic. The big bend that de Soto describes is where the root of the mountain projects outward, causing the river to have a distinctive U shape. That area is west of the downtown district of Chattanooga.

Brett flips through the pages of her book and studies the map. She uses her right index finger to trace the river and stops at the X she has penciled onto the map. This might be where de Soto landed. Brett looks up as Dr. Brown crests a ridge. Down below them is the city of Chattanooga. The fading sunlight glitters off the glass and metal facades of the buildings below. The tall buildings of downtown appear in the distance, sticking out of the ground like shining beacons reflecting the last rays of sunlight outward. The rays flash across the stone and trees on the flanks of the looming mountain. Lookout Mountain stretches toward the curving river at its base, as if seeking a long draught of the cooling water.

The SUV descends into the valley in seconds, and Brett feels her stomach rise into her throat as they lose elevation. Dr. Brown zips through the traffic, switching lanes around a few delivery trucks that have decided to ride a little too close together, creating a solid wall in the right lane. A sign stretching across the highway shows two diverging white arrows indicating a split in the road ahead. Chattanooga is on the right and Nashville is on the left.

Brett closes her book and places it in her pocket, where her dad's book is securely resting. She leans up in her seat so she can see their approach toward Chattanooga. Lookout Mountain doesn't look as tall as they move toward the split in the road. Brett looks up at the top of the mountain. There is a tower projecting upward from the east end. The waning rays of sunlight scatter as they collide with the structure. The light flashes out across the valley.

"Almost there," Natalie says a little apprehensively.

Brett looks over at her. Natalie extends her thumb and raises it into the air. It looks like her confidence is slowly returning. Brett places her thumb in the air and smiles. "Do you think the cross is there?" Natalie asks. "It has been hidden for five hundred years." Brett rubs the tip of her chin just like her dad does when she asks him difficult questions. She takes a few seconds to answer.

"Atohi told us to follow the path of de Soto," Brett says with confidence. "I think he knows that the cross is out here somewhere." Natalie rubs her hands against her pants, wiping away the sweat that is starting to form. Brett can see the nervousness in Natalie as she fidgets.

Brett's mind flashes to the image of Natalie hanging off the edge of the cliff in New Mexico. The terror on her face that day is an expression that she doesn't want to see again. Brett knows that the trackers will probably be searching for the cross as well, and that will lead them to the bend in the Tennessee River. She doesn't want anything to happen to Natalie or Grandpa Jake.

Brett can see that Natalie is probably thinking about the trackers finding them and gives her a reassuring smile. "We should be able to get in and get out long before the trackers find us," Brett says. "Hopefully we will have the cross and we can be on our way to Guasili." Natalie swallows and nods her head.

"Let's find that cross and get your dad back," Natalie says. She sets her jaw sternly and stares ahead out the windshield of the SUV. Her foot taps on the floor as they move closer and closer to the X on the map.

Doctor Brown merges into the slow lane. Cars speed by her as she slows down. The road splits, with two lanes heading off toward the base of the mountain and the other two lanes moving toward downtown. They round a curve and there, filling the windshield of the Escape, are the tall buildings of Chattanooga. As they pass the towering structures, a bright gold building catches the light of the sun and reflects it into the interior of the SUV. Brett shields her eyes as they drive by the shimmering structure.

"Where do we go now?" Dr. Brown asks.

"As soon as we cross the river, we need to get off the highway," Brett says.

The road is a winding black cord that roils through the tall buildings. Small hills with building complexes perched on the tops overlook the city center. On one of the hills, a large baseball stadium appears to have grown out of the earth. As they drive by the beautiful stadium, Brett can see the players running around in the outfield. A sign tells her that the Lookouts are home tonight. Game time 7:30. That is a little over an hour away.

The sight of the baseball stadium and the players playing brings a fleeting thought to her mind. The last time she listened to a game with her dad was the night before he was taken. She grits her teeth. She can't think about that now. She needs to stay focused on the task at hand. That is what her dad would do.

They finally pass the outfield wall and there in front of them is the slow-moving Tennessee River. Condominiums and houses line the bank of the river as the water continues its trek westward away from the city. Brett leans up in the seat and grabs the headrest in front of her. "There," she says, pointing out her window toward the west. There, below the mountain in the shadows caused by the fading sunlight, is the green plain that de Soto described. Brett can see the other ridge on the east side of the river. It appears as if the two ridges were pulled apart at some point in time, leaving this flat green surface behind.

Dr. Brown flexes her fingers on the steering wheel as she looks out the window. Grandpa Jake stirs from a long, road trip-induced nap, stretching his arms over his head and yawning loudly. "Glad you could join us, Grandpa Jake," Natalie says. Grandpa Jake wipes the sleep from his eyes as he looks out at the place Brett is pointing.

"Well, it looks like this terrain will be easier for an old man to navigate than the last place," he says.

The white SUV exits the highway and drops down to the riverside road. Dr. Brown turns left, and they travel between the condos that occupy both sides of the street. After two miles, they enter a much different landscape. The buildings have been replaced by long flat fields of tall grass. The brown heads sway from left to right in the late afternoon breeze. Brett glances out the back window. That has become a habit in the last few months. Looking over her shoulder to make sure that someone isn't chasing her.

"Which way?" Dr. Brown asks.

Brett turns and sees that the road comes to a stop. Another road that is just large enough for two cars to fit side by side branches off. The road to the right moves through thickets of trees as it trails off to the north. The road to the left moves through the same fields of orchard grass and tall fescue. The wind passes through the field like a wave as the tops ripple under the current.

Lookout Mountain looms at the end of the road to the left. It looks much higher down along the river. "Left," Brett says. Dr. Brown looks right, then left, and seeing nothing but plants and asphalt, pulls out onto the roadway. Brett can hear the gravel from the surface hitting the bottom of the SUV as the tires grip the loose debris. She glances behind her again just to make sure.

Brett sees that Natalie is tapping both feet on the floor, much faster than before. Brett looks ahead as the road ends at a tall clump of trees. Dr. Brown pulls the car into a gravel parking area and stops, pointing the front of the car toward the road. "Can't be too careful." The parking lot looks like a place where hikers park so they can take a walk along the river.

Brett quickly pulls out her field book and turns to the map of the area. She locates the X and looks at Natalie. "We will be fast," Brett says. She can see Natalie's fingers shaking. Natalie rubs her hands on her pants, trying to hide her nervousness.

"Let's do this," she says, flexing her fingers and grabbing the door handle.

"Keep close to each other," Dr. Brown says from the front seat. Natalie doesn't respond. She pushes the door open and jumps out, her feet crunching on the gravel as she walks. "Keep close!" Dr. Brown yells. Brett gets out of the SUV and steps on the coarse gravels that shift under her weight. Natalie hurries around the Escape toward her.

"Which way?" Natalie says as Dr. Brown and Grandpa Jake exit the vehicle.

Brett holds the book up close to her face. The light is beginning to fade as the sun moves further west. The shadows of the trees grow and migrate out over the SUV. Natalie takes out her phone and turns on the flashlight. "Thanks," Brett says as she looks up at the mountain towering over them and the tall trees hiding their path. Brett looks for topographical features that she can easily identify to point her toward the location of the ancient native village.

The X is sitting on a straight line from the point of Lookout Mountain to the apex of Stringer's Ridge to the northeast. Brett looks toward the ridges and moves to get in line with the spine of the ridge that is prominent in the distance. Then she turns and gets her body in alignment with the tip of Lookout Mountain. She glances backward, making sure she is still lined up. She extends her fingers outward and points with her whole hand like she is ready to do a karate chop. "This way." She walks toward the tall trees that bar their route to the river. Natalie runs up beside her, looking up at the trees and the darkening sky.

"We might have thirty minutes of light before it gets dark in there," she says, pointing at the forest.

"We will be out in plenty of time," Brett says confidently. "Don't lag, Grandpa."

Grandpa Jake hobbles along behind her. "Remember, keep close," Dr. Brown says. The trees on the bend are spaced evenly, giving them plenty of space to walk. They can also see further ahead. Brett gets glimpses of the broad river through the branches and leaves to the right. She wishes they were that close to their final destination, but they are headed toward the trough of the bend. Judging by the distance on the map, it should be another two hundred yards in front of them.

They continue through the shadows of the trees for another ten minutes. The trees thin and finally they emerge into a small clearing bordered by tall oaks and pines on every side. Brett looks up at the mountain above them. She is still in line with the point. She turns, but the spine of Stringer's Ridge isn't visible.

Brett hurries through the short grass and looks out at the river through the trees along the bank. She is certain that this is the flat position on the river that de Soto visited five hundred years ago. Brett looks around on the ground hurriedly, searching for some marker that would indicate the possible location of the cross. She makes a complete circle in the clearing, but there aren't any stones like the ones she found on the French Broad River.

"Look for a chevron or something like it around here," she says as she searches the ground with her flashlight. Natalie runs left and Grandpa Jake hobbles toward the right of the clearing. Dr. Brown searches in the area near where they emerged from the forest. Brett searches frantically as the last rays of sunlight crest the top of Lookout Mountain.

"This whole area looks like it has been disturbed," Grandpa Jake says as he walks over to stand beside her. He rubs the stubble on his chin. "What if the marker has been moved?"

Brett continues looking on the ground, but there is nothing.

"Nothing over here," Natalie yells.

"Nothing back here either," Dr. Brown says. Grandpa Jake puts his shaking hand on Brett's shoulder as she looks around the clearing.

"It has to be here," she says. "It just has to." Brett pulls herself away from Grandpa Jake and runs over to the edge of the trees along the riverbank. She looks up at the tall mountain. The wall of the mountain glistens as the light from the sun reflects off the water dripping from the rocks.

"It's not here," Brett says as she stares up at the sky.

"Maybe it is downriver," Dr. Brown says. "The river could have dislodged the marker at some point in the past."

"If that is the case, we will never find it," Natalie says.

Brett's shoulders slump as she looks down at the smooth, grassy clearing. She is sure the chevron marker is here at the bend of the river. She kicks a small brown pebble with her foot and sends it careening through the grass and into the fallen leaves on the ground. "What are we going to do now?" she asks softly. She walks out toward the water. The reflection of the mountain is visible on the surface.

"We should be getting out of here before you know who shows up," Natalie says.

"Come on, Brett," Grandpa Jake says. "We can head home and try another day."

Brett steps through the trees and leans against a tall oak that overhangs the slow-flowing water. The trunk of the tree is large enough that the four of them could link arms and they might make it all the way around. Brett is hidden from the others by the expanse of the oak's trunk. She stares out at the ripples on the water as the river slams into a large block of limestone that is almost submerged.

"Atohi told me to follow the path," she says.

Brett reaches down and picks up an angular rock the size of a golf ball and throws it into the water. She thought that would make her feel better, but it didn't. What is she going to do now? The link to her father is now broken. The chances of finding him and the entrance to the other city are getting slimmer by the second. "Hey, Brett!" she hears Grandpa Jake yelling. "It's time to go."

Brett kneels at the base of the oak tree. She can feel the tears starting to form. She has fought hard over the last few months to keep them bottled up inside her. Her dad would not want her crying about failing. He would want her to continue down the path ahead of her. He would want her to figure it out for herself. He would want her to solve the problem in front of her and finish the quest.

But she feels that she can't be that strong. She can't focus on a solution any longer. The warm tears leak from her blue eyes down her cheeks. They flow in torrents. She places her face in her hands and releases all the frustration and loss there by the slow-moving water.

"Why are you crying?" a soft voice whispers.

Brett jumps off the ground and falls against the tree. Standing in front of her is a tall man with dark eyes and long black hair pulled back in a long ponytail. He holds his finger to his mouth asking her to remain silent. "What you search for is not here," he whispers. The man kneels and draws an X in the dirt. "It has left our realm, but the energy that it possesses creates a ripple in space and time."

Brett watches the man as he draws the X. His eyes sparkle like diamonds as he looks up at her. His motions and his speech remind her of Atohi. "Atohi?" she whispers.

He cocks his head to the side and smiles. "He is one of us, yes."

Brett shakes her head and wipes the tears from her face. "How?" she asks.

"I cannot stay long," he says, "but while here I will point you in the direction of the ripple." He picks up a small pebble and drops it into the water. "Just like the rock creating a ripple in the water, the cross creates a ripple, and you must find that ripple if you want to locate the cross."

Brett shakes her head, trying to comprehend what he is saying. Behind her, she can hear Grandpa Jake calling out. "Brett, you alright?" The man looks behind her in the direction of her grandfather.

"On my way," Brett says.

The man traces a curving line on the ground. The pattern resembles the line of a river on a map. The man points down at the undulating line. "The cross was taken through the gorge toward the setting sun," he whispers again. "Out of our reach. You must find it if you wish to find Gausili." She leans down and looks at the curved line.

"So, continue west?" Brett asks, glancing up at his face. He nods.

"Brett, come on now!" Grandpa Jake yells.

"It's getting dark," Natalie says. "You said to get in and get out."

Brett can hear the crunching of leaves and turns quickly. Grandpa Jake and Natalie walk out from under the oak trees and stop when they see her. "What are you doing?" Natalie asks. "What did you draw that for?" She points at the drawing on the ground. Brett turns around. The man who was talking with her has vanished.

"What?" Brett says as she walks over to the edge of the river and looks up and down the bank. "Where?"

Natalie walks over and looks in the same direction. "Did you find anything?" she asks.

"You all were right," Brett says. "It isn't here. But I think I can figure out where it is." Brett starts toward the clearing. She grabs Grandpa Jake by the hand. "Come on, Grandpa." He turns and walks beside her.

"I didn't make it this far without your help," Grandpa Jake says with a smile.

"I know, Grandpa."

The stars are bright in the dark sky as they stride out into the clearing. "Heading home?" Dr. Brown says. Brett stops in front of her.

"We have one stop to make first," she says.

"I knew it. I knew it," Natalie says. "Where are we heading this time?"

Brett smiles. "West," she says as she walks with Grandpa Jake toward the trees lining the grassy clearing.

CHAPTER 10

Memphis Morning

It is well after midnight when Dr. Brown drives the SUV into Hernando, Mississippi. "I think we should stop here," she says, rubbing her eyes. Grandpa Jake is asleep in the front seat. The deep tones of his snoring remind Brett of the sounds a kid makes when playing the tuba for the first time. Natalie stifles her laughter by placing her hand firmly over her mouth.

"You know, you can almost dance to this," Natalie whispers as she taps her feet on the floor. That causes Brett to laugh harder, and she too places her hand over her mouth so as to not wake up her grandfather.

They both laugh uncontrollably, with their hands over their mouths and their whole bodies shaking rapidly. Natalie opens her mouth as if she is the one snoring. Brett grips her mouth tighter. It is good to laugh like this again. Just to be a normal eleven-year-old is quite refreshing. The thoughts of Cibola, de Soto, a cross, and the trackers are far from her mind at this moment.

The girls grow louder in the back seat as they can no longer hold in their laughter. Grandpa Jake stirs and lets out another, more robust sound that causes them to giggle all over again. Water leaks out of Brett's eyes as she takes her hands off her mouth and lets the laugher spill from her.

She looks out the window, wiping the tears from her eyes. They pass by City Hall Cheesecake. Brett's stomach gurgles and growls. A slice of cheesecake sounds good right now. As they drive by the DeSoto County Museum, Brett stops laughing entirely. The sight of the Spanish-style building, with its illuminated arched doorway, causes the reason for their trip west to push aside the frivolity. Brett rubs her hands on her cargo pants, transferring her tears to the brown fabric.

Natalie looks over at her still, shaking uncontrollably as Grandpa Jake continues snoring. Brett stares down at her hands as they move slowly against the rough material. "Hey," Natalie whispers. Brett glances up and Natalie once again mimics Grandpa Jake, but Brett doesn't laugh.

Dr. Brown pulls into a dimly lit parking lot. The sign out front says this is the Commerce Inn. It is a brick building that looks like a motel from the late sixties. There is a small square building in front of the inn with white letters telling everyone that it is a restaurant. The light under the *t* is flashing like it is ready to burn out. Dr. Brown parks the car, and they all stare up at the peeling white paint and the exposed red bricks beneath. "We aren't staying here, are we?" Natalie asks with her nose scrunched together. "Bet there are bed bugs, and no telling what else in there."

Dr. Brown turns around, letting out a large yawn. "I can't drive another mile," she says.

Brett looks at the rustic building. She is sure that it was nice fifty years ago, but the years have been unkind. She yawns. It is the first time since they left Chattanooga that she has felt fatigued. Studying the maps in her book and reading and rereading the descriptions on Dr. Hall's drawing kept her going. Then, reading the letters she found in her dad's desk from the unknown author kept the fuel of discovery going, pushing the idea of sleep far from her, but now she welcomes it. She can use a few hours when her mind isn't racing.

"Sounds good, Dr. Brown," Brett says.

"Thank you."

Natalie looks over at Brett, her nose still scrunched together. "I thought you were my friend," she says.

"I am," Brett says as she opens the door. "I know how much you like scary movies, and this place has that feel to it."

"Ha, ha," Natalie replies. "Bed bugs and a person lurking inside the vent."

"Hope you can sleep," Brett says as she grabs her bag and steps out of the car.

Brett closes the door and walks around the SUV. She opens the passenger door and delicately touches Grandpa Jake on the shoulder. "We're here, Grandpa." He slowly opens his eyes, then widens them as he sees Brett staring down at him. "Dr. Brown found us a nice place to stay for the night," Brett continues.

Grandpa Jake rubs his eyes and sits up. "Lead the way," he says. Brett helps him out of the SUV and they walk toward the dilapidated brick building to get a room.

* * * * *

Morning arrives a little too early for Brett as sunlight filters into the small room through a grimy windowpane. She is laying on top of the covers with Grandpa Jake snoring softly beside her. She looks at the clock beside the bed. The red numbers on the face can't be right; it can't be 6:45. She rolls off the bed. She is still wearing the clothes from yesterday, and she has her shoes on. Just like Natalie, she is being cautious.

She walks on the tips of her shoes across the orange shag carpet. She isn't sure why she is tiptoeing across the room when the thick carpet muffles the sounds of her steps anyway. She sits down on an old, rickety wooden chair that sits in front of a weathered wooden table. The chair squeaks loudly under her weight. She glances back toward the twin beds, making sure Natalie and the others are still asleep. None of the others move as she scoots herself closer to the table. She opens her bag and takes out her field books.

Brett places the wrinkled pages of the books in front of her on the scratched surface of the table. "De Soto," she whispers, "where are you?" The descriptions led her to Memphis, but now she needs to find the location of the cross. The words of the Nunnehi echo inside her head as she stares at the map showing the path of de Soto. *The cross will transmit a signal like a ripple on the water.* Brett sits back and rubs her chin between her thumb and finger.

"Transmit a signal like a ripple on the water," she says softly. That sounds like a wave. Maybe the cross transmits waves like S and P waves from an earthquake. The primary and secondary waves released during an earthquake propagate outward from the source. So, the cross is the focus, and the ripples are the energy waves. "How am I going to find the center of this energy source?" she whispers. She leans back in the chair and places her hands behind her head. "How do they know an earthquake happens? Aside from the shaking and everything falling off your walls." She looks up at the stained yellow ceiling.

"A seismograph," she says a little too loudly. That is how they find the location of an earthquake. That is how they measure the intensity of the energy released during the event. "I need the readout from a seismograph."

"Talking to yourself again," Natalie says as she sits down beside her in the other rickety chair. "Waking up the entire room. I'm not going to forgive you this time." She looks at the books on the table. "Looks like you're deciding where we should go next." Brett looks absently at the maps in front of her.

"I know you can hear me," Natalie continues.

"We need a seismograph," Brett says without looking up.

"Is that all?"

"You remember me telling you what the Nunnehi said about the cross?"

"It transmits energy or something," Natalie says.

"Energy waves, just like an earthquake," Brett says slowly.

Brett pushes the books into the center of the table and leans back in the chair. It screeches as the slats and legs shift under her weight. "You think a seismograph can pick up the waves?" Brett nods as she runs her fingers through her blonde hair.

"Should work," she says.

Natalie stares at her with her mouth open. "Okay. But there aren't too many places that have Richter scales just laying around."

Brett looks at her with a broad smile. "The University of Memphis isn't far from here, and they use the CERI network to study the New Madrid fault."

"Oh."

"They study that fault continually, and I bet the signal from the cross shows up in the seismograph tape."

"We need to see that tape, don't we?" Natalie asks.

"That is where your mom can be a big help," Brett says. "She can get us into the university so we can see it."

"Shall I wake them up?" Natalie says.

"It is only seven. We have some time, and besides, they probably could use another thirty minutes."

Natalie nods as she taps her foot nervously on the thick carpet. The table shakes slightly with each movement. Brett looks over at Grandpa Jake as he sleeps soundly through his soft snores. He needs at least another thirty minutes considering where he has been over the last few days. He has hiked with her up ridges and steep slopes in north-eastern Tennessee. He hiked with her at the bend, and she isn't sure where the seismograph will lead them next. She needs him rested and ready to go when it is time. The cross is out there . . . and so are the trackers.

Natalie is staring at her with the worried look she gets when she knows things are about to get intense. "Will this be the end of the road?" she asks.

Brett runs her fingers through her hair again. "Once we have the cross, we should be able to find the entrance to the city," Brett says. Natalie nods.

"Hope we find it fast. I don't want to meet the trackers when we're looking for it."

Brett shakes her head. "Neither do I." Brett grabs her books and places them in the bag. She can feel the excitement building inside of her. The accumulating energy feels like it is ready to split her chest open. She takes a few deep breaths to calm herself. *This is it*. The cross is within her reach, and she is going to find it and use it to locate her dad.

* * * * *

Dr. Brown has them at the University of Memphis punctually at eleven o'clock. They have a meeting with Professor Bergenbek, the lead researcher of seismic activity on the New Madrid fault. He seemed very polite on the phone and a bit excited that a few middle school students were researching the energy build-up and release along the fault.

Brett walks beside Dr. Brown down the stairs to the research facility. The campus isn't too crowded during the last few weeks of summer break, but the research building is different. Researchers are walking up the stairs carrying rolls of paper with red and black lines scribbled on them. Brett catches sight of a man in his early twenties with a pencil behind his ear reading a chart as he walks up the steps. He doesn't notice them as they pass, but Brett gets a good view of the chart. The squiggly lines form tall peaks and deep valleys, and there are two distinct sets of lines.

"The first lines are the P waves," Dr. Brown says in a whisper.

"The second is the S wave," Brett replies. "They travel at two-point-two miles per second and cause most of the damage during an earthquake."

"Now you're just showing off," Natalie says with a huff.

"You are the daughter of a geologist," Dr. Brown says.

"Those wave patterns are going to help us locate the cross," Brett says.

"New Madrid is a busy fault," Dr. Brown replies. "It might be difficult to pinpoint a small undulating electrical signal along the fault line."

"It's out there, I am sure of that," Brett says.

"Rock said that when he proposed an expedition for Cibola."

"He found it, and I am finding the cross."

Brett looks up at Dr. Brown with absolute confidence. Brett knows it is out there, but she needs Professor Bergenbek and Dr. Brown to help locate the small ripples in the system. With their expertise, the cross will be found. They continue down the stairs until they step out into a well-lit corridor. A man with a thick red beard that reaches his shirt collar is standing in the center of the room, carefully massaging his beard as he watches them enter. He smiles broadly and walks over toward them, still stroking his bushy beard.

"Dr. Brown, it is good to see you again," Professor Bergenbek says in a deep, Santa-like voice. He stretches his vast hand out, ready to shake Dr. Brown's arms off. Dr. Brown extends her hand and shakes with plenty of force that it surprises the professor. "As strong as ever." He laughs heartily, shaking his whole body. He eyes Brett and Natalie. "So, these are the young researchers you have brought?" he says with his thick red eyebrows raised.

Professor Bergenbek holds out his large hand and Brett and Natalie each shake it. "Now," he says, "you are looking for a low-frequency energy wave." He looks intently at Brett, then moves on to Natalie, and then settles on Dr. Brown. "This is some advanced research you have here. I pulled the data from our vast array of seismic data. Follow me and we will have some fun with the machines." Professor Bergenbek turns and ambles down the wide hallway.

He stops in front of a large oak door. The sign on the door tells those that enter that this is the Center for Earthquake Research. He turns, smiling. "This should be exciting." He pushes the door open. "This room is extraordinary." He leads them into a room filled with large, spinning drums. There are computer banks along the left side of the room, and on the right side, there are printing machines producing papers with the squiggly lines on them.

Brett walks over and holds one of the pieces of paper in her hand. She studies the two distinctive wave patterns, first the P waves and then the S waves. This one must have just happened, but she didn't feel it. There is more than one machine printing out wave patterns simultaneously.

Natalie walks over and stands beside her, looking at the machines as they whir and whine. "This place is insane." Brett stares at the information printing rapidly on the long pieces of paper.

"This is going to be harder than I thought," she says, grimacing.

Natalie shakes her head. "Isn't science always harder than you think?"

Brett feels her chest tighten, as if a large weight is pressing down upon her as she watches the lines speed across the page. How could she think she was just going to walk into the research facility and instantly find the anomaly? It seems impossible that they will find the ripple today, and they might not find it at all. Brett turns and makes eye contact with Grandpa Jake. He has remained silent the entire time they have been inside the research center. He nods slowly, letting her know she can do this.

Professor Bergenbek walks over, rubbing his beard. "This is a little overwhelming, I know," he says. "What I have to show you is more manageable." He leads them through the aisles of computers and walks into a smaller, quieter room. He closes the door after they are all inside. The whirring and whining stop.

"When you called, Dr. Brown, looking for minor electrical signals, I was somewhat perplexed, but I ran the information through our database and I was astonished by the results."

Dr. Bergenbek takes three rolls of paper from the long wooden table on the back wall and rolls them out. Brett, Natalie, and Dr. Brown walk over and look down at the seismograph display. There are a series of lines in wave-like patterns drawn in black ink on the white rolls of paper. There are ten sets of lines, with the P waves appearing first and then the S waves. All the drawings appear similar except for the last group.

On the last seismograph is a much smaller wave pattern that shows both waves overlapping and appearing to be the same. Professor Bergenbek strokes his thick red beard. "These two lines shouldn't be here, and they shouldn't be appearing at the same time."

"Why are they like that?" Brett asks.

"We thought it might be interference," Professor Bergenbek says thoughtfully. "They appeared on a number of our stations." He pulls out the next set of drawings and there on the page is the same pattern. "Again, these seismic waves should not be doing that," Professor Bergenbek says, running his fingers through his beard. "There should be a gap in the waves."

Dr. Brown leans down over the printout. "They don't appear to be seismic waves at all," she says, looking up at the professor. He nods repeatedly.

"It is odd, to say the least."

Brett stares at the patterns on the pages. "How far back do these signals appear?" she asks. Brett finds herself holding her breath as she awaits the response. Professor Bergenbek tilts his head to the side and studies her face. A small curl forms on his lip.

"That is the extraordinary component of all the data from these testing sites. They are there every time."

Brett takes her Royals hat off her head and runs her fingers through her blonde hair. "Hidden in plain sight," she exclaims.

Professor Bergenbek chuckles and slaps his right leg with his hand. "Dr. Brown, you have a very bright student here."

Dr. Brown nods in agreement. "What testing sites registered these wave patterns?"

Professor Bergenbek shuffles around and takes a black folder from the desk. He opens the front cover and looks down at the printed letters. "We can triangulate it using the station here and one in Little Rock and the other in Birmingham to help us find the location of this signal." Brett looks down at the drawing. She can feel the blood rushing through her veins as she hears the professor's words.

Natalie steps next to Brett and looks at her. "You were right," she whispers. "I really shouldn't doubt you anymore." Brett places her index finger to her lips, telling Natalie to be quiet. Natalie covers her mouth with her left hand and nods.

Professor Bergenbek smiles broadly. "When we triangulated the signals, the point where they overlapped was near Greenville Mississippi." Brett quickly takes out her field book and turns to the map she has drawn of de Soto's journey. She pulls her black pencil from her pocket and places an X over Greenville. Her fingers twitch nervously over her mouth as she thinks about the final resting place of the cross.

De Soto died of a fever in 1542, and his men placed him in a hollow log and dropped him in the Mississippi River. *What if he never let the cross go? What if it is in the hollowed-out log with him?* If she found the resting place of de Soto, that would be another fantastic find. The cross *and* the final resting place of Hernando de Soto would be quite an achievement.

She couldn't think about the accolades or the praise she would receive. "Finding Dad is the single most important goal," she says to herself. She shoves the book into her pocket and looks up at Professor Bergenbek. "Thank you for all your help, Professor."

He laughs. "I wish all my students could see things like you do, young lady." Brett looks down at the table. She never really liked compliments.

"Hope you apply here after you graduate," he continues. "The University of Memphis would be happy to have you." Brett keeps her eyes focused on the table.

"Thank you," she says.

Dr. Brown holds out her hand. "Thanks for your help."

Professor Bergenbek nods. "My pleasure. Can I ask one question before you leave?"

"Of course," says Dr. Brown.

"What is transmitting those signals?"

"Aliens," Natalie says smiling.

"Natalie," Dr. Brown replies.

"We aren't sure, but we think it is a kind of resonance bar," Brett says.

"A resonance bar?" Professor Bergenbek asks, not fully understanding.

"A bar that can locate certain electrical anomalies in space," Dr. Brown says.

Professor Bergenbek's eyes narrow. "I see. I never would have guessed there is a transmitter buried in the sediments at the bottom of the river. One that can locate electrical anomalies. That is mind-blowing. Let me know if you find it." He shakes his head. Brett looks up.

"We will." Brett turns and walks toward the door. She grabs Grandpa Jake by the arm as she walks up to him. "You were quiet," she says.

He scratches the stubble on the side of his face. "Figured I would let you work without me getting in the way."

"You never get in the way, Grandpa," Brett says as they open the door. The whirring and whining of the printing machines fill the air, but Professor Bergenbek's voice booms over the chirping of the machines.

"Good luck," he says as he runs his fingers through his long beard. "Oh, and you might need this." He walks toward them, holding a small device that looks like a walkie-talkie. "This will help locate small electrical frequencies." He holds it out for Brett and the others to see. "Hold this button down to actuate the sensor, and this antenna receives the signal," he says, pushing the button on the side of the machine.

"Thank you," Dr. Brown says. "This will help us find the needle in the haystack."

A broad smile spreads across Professor Bergenbek's face as he looks at Brett. "This should find whatever is out there. Just bring it back so I can see what we've been seeing all these years." Brett nods and walks out, arm in arm with Grandpa Jake.

Next stop, Greenville, Mississippi.

CHAPTER 11

Trouble with Time

D r. Brown drove south from Memphis to Greenville as fast as Brett has ever seen her drive. Brett has the sense that Dr. Brown is excited about locating the final resting place of Hernando de Soto. Brett understands. Her heart starts racing even before they drive through downtown Greenville. Her pulse started quickening immediately after they left the university.

The three-hour drive south along Highway 278 took way too long. The endless rows of cotton swaying in the fields didn't help time speed up. Fortunately, they are in Greenville now, and they can begin the process of finding the final resting place of de Soto. Brett looks over at Natalie, sitting beside her in the back seat. Natalie is tapping her right leg and switching to tapping her left leg. Her lips move as she appears to be timing her taps to some song that Brett can't hear.

Dr. Brown drives west toward the river. They drive for another five minutes and suddenly the wide, muddy, slow-moving water of the Mississippi River comes into view. The gentle roll of the water along the bank is mesmerizing. The wide channel of the river poses a daunting task: locating the hollowed-out log that was used to bury de Soto. How are they going to find something so small in a channel so wide and long?

"I see the wheels turning," Natalie says.

"This puzzle is a little daunting, don't you think?" Brett asks.

"Nah," Natalie says. "We always figure things out. But it does look like we might need a boat for this part of the journey."

"Looks that way," Brett says.

Dr. Brown looks into the rearview mirror, her eyes darting from Brett to Natalie and back to the road. "Should be able to rent one at the marina. I saw a sign a few miles back."

Natalie rubs her hands together. "How are we going to get the cross out of the river?" Brett hasn't thought about that, and it makes her just a little angry. She should have thought about it.

"We have the electrical receiver to find the spot. Once we have the location, we can focus on the retrieval," Dr. Brown says.

"Retrieval means somebody is going down underwater to get it," Natalie says with a worried look on her face.

That is something else Brett hasn't thought about. How could she have been so thoughtless? All of these things should have been arranged before she arrived in Greenville. Her dad always planned for the expedition. He had everything that he could need. She isn't living up to the standard at the moment.

"Retrieval is secondary right now," Dr. Brown says. "Locate first. Mark it and then return when we have the right equipment." Dr. Brown is looking at Brett, her brown eyes wide. Brett nods.

"I think that is best, considering our situation," Brett says. Grandpa Jake turns and smiles. At least he isn't disappointed in her lack of preparation.

* * * * *

Brett is standing on the front deck of a red and green pontoon boat, looking out at the ripples on the water. She has the electrical meter in her hand and is listening intently to the pings as they move south down the river. The breeze feels cool and refreshing on her sweat-soaked skin as they cut through the choppy water. The outboard engine makes a shrill sound as Dr. Brown pushes the throttle forward. The sediment-filled water of the

Mississippi River splashes up on deck as the boat rocks backward and forward on the wakes from a passing barge filled with large chunks of coal. Dr. Brown holds tightly to the wheel as she steers down the right side of the wide channel.

Natalie stands beside Brett, looking down at the small metallic instrument with its antenna outstretched toward the horizon. "Do you think we can find the electrical signal with that?" Natalie asks with her brow furrowed.

Brett doesn't take her eyes off the horizon. "We found the magnetic field in New Mexico with something this size," she says confidently. "We are going to find the cross with this." The small pings sound like someone tapping a glass with their fingernail.

They travel up and down the river, making passes along a grid-like pattern. Brett quickly draws the grid on her map and pencils in the GPS coordinates using her cell phone. The map of the river looks like a series of boxes. Some of the boxes have red Xs drawn through them; the others have light penciled checkmarks. Every time there is a ping transmitted by the device, Brett checks the appropriate box.

They have been on the water for over three hours and the air is thick and sticky with the afternoon humidity. "I hope we find it quick," Natalie says, wiping the sweat off her brow. "It feels like I'm breathing through a wet blanket." Brett holds the electrical meter in her hand tightly. Her Royals cap has turned a dark blue color from the absorbed sweat. The sweat trickles down her face and she wipes it away from her eyes. *Ping.* She glances down at her map. She makes a light check. The row beside this one has all red Xs.

Five seconds later there is another *ping.* That is the first time they have occurred in rapid succession. Brett looks down at the machine, puzzled. *Ping.* Another. And then very rapidly, *ping, ping, ping.* Brett holds her hand high up in the air. That is the signal for Dr. Brown to stop. *Ping, ping, ping.* Natalie turns toward Dr. Brown. "Stop!" she yells. "We have something up here!"

The boat lurches forward as Dr. Brown pulls back on the throttle, stopping their forward motion. The boat bobs up and down on the waves like a corked bottle in the ocean. *Ping, ping, ping.* Brett's heart is beating so fast against her ribcage it feels like it is ready to break free from its restraints. Her mouth is dry. She looks down at the dial as it moves quickly from right to left. "Looks like this might be it!" Brett yells.

She looks back at Grandpa Jake. He is sitting in the seat next to Dr. Brown. He smiles at her and nods slowly. Brett rubs her hands together, takes the pencil from behind her ear, and marks a check on the map. They are about ten miles south of Greenville. There isn't much in the way of landmarks on this stretch of the Mississippi River. Along the bank is just field after field of cotton. Brett takes out a buoy marker that they brought to set in the river when they found the location of the cross.

The water laps at the sides of the two silver pontoons as Brett and Natalie attach an electrical transmitter to the buoy. Grandpa Jake hobbles to the front of the boat, picks up the heavy anchor and throws it into the water. Muddy water splashes onto the deck—and onto Natalie. "Thanks, Grandpa Jake," she says as she finishes tying the small square transmitter firmly to the plastic buoy. Grandpa Jake chuckles as he shuffles back to the rear of the boat.

Ping, ping, ping. Brett picks up the buoy and walks to the edge of the boat. The up and down motion makes it feel like her stomach is in her throat. She turns on the transmitter, and the receiver immediately picks up the signal with a smaller *ping* in between the larger *pings.* "Receiving both signals. Well done building this on such short notice, Dr. Brown," Brett says.

"Thank goodness it works," Dr. Brown replies.

Brett leans over the side and delicately places the buoy into the water. It rises and falls with the flow of the wake on the river. "Shouldn't have any trouble finding this spot tomorrow," Brett says as she sits up on her knees. The boat rocks back and forth much faster than it has before. The rocking is so violent that it almost throws Natalie off her feet. Brett looks around for the source of the dangerous wake.

A large lake cruiser with a towering deck is racing toward them pushing columns of water out behind. The wakes rock the buoys that indicate the channel violently from left to right. Brett scrambles toward the back of the boat. "They've found us!" she yells. The wide white boat pulls up alongside the pontoon boat, causing it to rock violently. Water splashes onto the deck, spraying Natalie with brown droplets. In the back of the boat, Dr. Brown tries pushing the throttle forward. The engine sputters, spits, and whines.

"A perfect time for technical difficulties," Natalie yells.

The large lake cruiser bangs into the side of the pontoon boat. Brett slams into the rails so hard she almost falls over the side into the churning Mississippi, but the force of the hit sends her falling to the deck. She rubs her shoulder as she shakes her head back and forth, trying to regain her clarity. She sees Grandpa Jake face down on the slippery deck, grasping for her. She searches frantically for Natalie and sees her sitting against the cover for the boat, pointing at the towering side of the massive cruiser.

The cruiser grinds against the metallic pontoons, causing an earsplitting noise like nails on a chalkboard. Brett rocks backward and forward until she can feel her lunch starting to move up her throat from her stomach. She swallows hard, forcing the acidic mixture back down, and scrambles to her feet. The deck shifts from right to left underneath her as the pontoon boat rises and falls on the enormous wake.

Brett stumbles over to Grandpa Jake and grabs his arm. Suddenly three loud *thunks* cause Brett to turn. "This is getting worse!" Natalie yells. Three men wearing blue coveralls land on the deck of the swaying pontoon boat. With their cropped hair and pressed clothes they look like they could be members of the United States Navy.

Each man is carrying a small, snub-nosed revolver, and they are pointing them at Brett, Natalie, and Dr. Brown. Ropes fall onto the deck of the pontoon boat, and two other men jump down onto the deck and tie the two vessels together. They move along the floor of the rising and falling vessel with ease. They appear to be accustomed to life on the water and tie their knots quickly.

Brett glances at Natalie. She is still sitting on the floor, leaning against the boat cover with her arms up in the air. Brett looks around, trying to figure out how they can escape. Her bag is sitting under the bench seat, but there isn't anything in there that can help them against armed men. They have an anchor, but unfortunately it has already been thrown into the water. This is one time that she might have to let go and see where events take her. She looks down at Grandpa Jake. He grimaces. She can see the pain from the fall ripple through the creases of his face. He squeezes her hand lightly and stands up.

Brett's shoulders slump as she stares at the strong men pointing their guns at them. A loud voice cuts through the silence of the moment—a syrupy voice that she recognizes instantly. "That wasn't a very nice thing to do. Leaving us up on that mountain," Dr. Hall says, leaning over the silver railing of the lake cruiser. Her wide-brimmed hat shades her eyes as she rubs her hands together rapidly. "But as you can see, things do work out the way they should. Bring them aboard."

The two men who tied the boats together walk slowly toward Dr. Brown and pull her away from the controls. They push her across the swaying deck toward a yellow rope ladder that has been thrown down from the top of the cruiser. The other three men with the pistols motion for Brett and Grandpa Jake to move over to the ladder. Brett holds onto Grandpa Jake as they walk across the swaying deck. "Don't be so pushy," Natalie says as she stumbles across the deck and crashes into Brett. "Sorry."

"What are you going to do with us?" Brett yells up toward Dr. Hall.

"I think I will treat you much better than you treated me. That is certain."

"You could let us go," Brett continues.

"Can't do that," Dr. Hall says with a giggle. "You see, you have something I want."

"I don't have anything," Brett says angrily.

Brett can feel the blood rushing into her face, causing her skin to increase in temperature. The heat of Mississippi in late summer might be helping that as well. She glares at the smiling face of Dr. Hall. "Bring them up. We can have a more civilized talk about what you are going to do for me," she says sweetly before turning abruptly and disappearing behind the metal railing.

Dr. Brown climbs up the flimsy rope ladder first as the sailors prod her forward. Once she reaches the top, a pair of hands grab her and pull her from view. Natalie glances over at Brett with her jaw set firmly. "Don't help that witch with anything." Brett nods. Natalie scampers up the rope like a lemur in a tree. Next Grandpa Jake climbs slowly up the rolling ladder, followed by Brett.

Brett climbs over the rail and studies the deck. Grandpa Jake, Natalie, and Dr. Brown are standing in the middle of the polished wooden floor, looking at the line of eight men with revolvers pointed at them. "Over here if you please, Miss Wilson,"

Dr. Hall says. She motions for Brett to stand next to Grandpa Jake. These men look just like the ones who came aboard their vessel. Each of them has dark eyes and they seem to lack any sense of emotion—like robots. No smiles. Nothing.

Brett walks over and stands beside Grandpa Jake. "How are you?" she whispers.

He leans close to her ear. "Fine. You see any way out of this yet?" Brett shakes her head slowly so Dr. Hall won't notice. "Keep your eyes open," he says through the side of his mouth.

Dr. Hall walks down the steps from the cabin of the large cruiser holding, onto the brightly stained wooden rail. She pauses a few seconds between each step, making sure Brett and the others focus on her. "Well, I can say that I am glad we are back together," she says kindly. Brett remains focused on her as she takes another step. "We almost had you in Chattanooga," she continues. "You have become quite elusive." She steps down on the wooden deck and places her hands on her hips. "But here we are, at the final resting place of de Soto."

Brett glares at her with narrowed eyes. Dr. Hall smiles wider. "You are a very good explorer," she says. "Just like your father." Brett didn't think Dr. Hall knew her dad. After all, he is a professor in the geology department, and she is a professor in the history department. The question gnaws at her insides as she glares at the soft, sinister smile on Dr. Hall's face.

"I knew your father very well," she says sweetly, "In fact, I helped him translate some of Esteban's writings. Only small details, but I did assist. And that bit of information I gathered helped me formulate a truly remarkable idea." Dr. Hall takes three steps forward and stops six feet in front of Brett. She places her hands on her hips and cocks her head to the right. She surveys Brett's face intently. "The stories of Esteban resembled the account of Ortiz, and that meant there was another location. One that the tribes in the southeast describe in their writings. One that de Soto found."

"Gausili," Brett whispers.

"Precisely."

"When you disappeared on that ridge, I thought my chance for finding Gausili was over. How was I going to find the riches of Gausili? You were the key."

"Why did you need me?" Brett asks softly.

"You had the map and a key to guide you. I got a glimpse of it when you showed me your map and research."

"How did you know we would be here?"

"If de Soto had it, then it would be resting with him in his tomb. And Clarke did point me in this direction. Unfortunately, he is entombed just like de Soto."

Dr. Hall spreads her arms wide and motions to the area around the boat. "Here we are," she says. Brett glances over at Grandpa Jake. She had thought Clarke Daly was just as bad as Dr. Hall, but now it looks like she will do anything for the riches of Gausili. Grandpa Jake moves closer to Brett so that their shoulders are almost touching. "We are bringing de Soto back to the surface today," Dr. Hall says. She motions to one of her navy henchmen. A man with light brown hair and a scar over his left eyes walks over with black scuba tanks in his hand. He places them in front of Dr. Hall before heading back to the rear of the boat. He returns with more scuba gear.

Brett looks at the scuba gear. *At least they were prepared.* Dr. Hall laughs. "Always be prepared for anything during an expedition," she says. "Your dad taught me that." Brett grits her teeth together. She doesn't like hearing about her dad and Dr. Hall discussing treasure hunting trips. That was reserved for her. "As you can see, I am prepared to bring the wooden coffin of de Soto up." The anger builds inside Brett as she watches Dr. Hall walk confidently in front of them.

"You and your goon squad are going to have a hard time locating de Soto." Brett says. "No visibility, and a coffin that has been in the river for over four hundred years. A needle in a hundred haystacks is easier to find."

Natalie steps forward with her head held high. "That's right. No way you find it." Dr. Hall slowly turns her head and looks at Natalie. The broad smile never leaves her face.

"We will find the cross," she says confidently.

Brett doesn't like the sound of this. She clenches her fists together, her fingernails digging into the flesh in the palms of her hands. Dr. Hall points a manicured finger toward Brett. "You're coming with us, silly," she says with a laugh. "And you're bringing your fancy little electrometer." The air rushes out of Brett's lungs as she hears the words. She doesn't want to go anywhere with Dr. Hall, but diving down to the bottom of the Mississippi River with her is the last place she wants to go with her. *How does she know about the electrometer?*

She motions for the men with guns to move forward. "Get your gear on," she says in a pleasant voice as the men point their guns toward them. Brett looks at Grandpa Jake.

"She isn't going anywhere with you," Grandpa Jake spits.

Dr. Hall steps toward Grandpa Jake. "She will, or you will be the first one to die, and then your friend." She snaps her fingers and the man behind them presses the barrel of the gun into Grandpa Jake's back. "I don't want to do that though," Dr. Hall says. "I would prefer to remain civilized."

"Alright," Brett says.

Dr. Hall claps her hands together and laughs. "This is going to be so much fun." Brett looks up at Grandpa Jake. His eyes are wide with fear, and Brett is sure it is fear for her. Brett walks over and picks up a set of scuba gear. "It is a good thing Rock taught you how to dive," Dr. Hall says with a smirk on her face. "But I am not heartless. Dr. Brown, you will accompany us." She has her hands clasped tightly in front of her as she eyes Dr. Brown.

Dr. Brown turns her head slowly toward Natalie. "It will be alright, Mom," Natalie says confidently. "Watch over Brett."

"Who is going to watch over you?"

"Grandpa Jake, of course."

Dr. Brown hugs Natalie and walks over to the pile of scuba gear. "That was touching." Dr. Hall wipes the edges of her eyes. "Now, time for discovery. Let's find de Soto," she says, clapping her hands together.

CHAPTER 12

Raising the Coffin

Brett is standing next to Dr. Brown on the polished wooden deck near the stern of Dr. Hall's boat with a pair of air tanks on her back. The weight of the load causes her to hunch over slightly. The brown water splashes up on the boards as it hits the edge of the boat. Dr. Brown places her hand on Brett's shoulder. Brett knows Dr. Brown will keep her safe. Lined up behind them are Dr. Hall and four of her dark-clothed henchmen.

Brett has the electrometer in her hands. It is beeping lightly. She pulls her mask over her eyes and presses it tightly to her face, her fingers shaking slightly. It has been over a year since she has been on a diving trip. Her dad took her to Peacock Springs in Florida. She thought it was really neat to see the depressions in the limestone where the water had continually weathered the rock and transported it somewhere else. Her PADI junior open water dive license allows her to drive down to forty feet, and her dad always made sure their dives never exceeded that depth.

Brett looks over the metal railing at the slow-moving river. She is sure that where they are going is far beyond the forty-foot depth. A lump forms in her throat as she gazes down at the churning water. This isn't going to be anything like the cave dives with her dad. This is dangerous . . . life-threatening. Dr. Brown squeezes her shoulder tighter. Brett looks up at her through her foggy mask. She can feel the fright flowing through Dr. Brown's fingers into her shoulders, like an energy pulse that transfers with every beat of her heart.

Brett takes a deep breath to calm herself and starts to count backward from ten. *Ten, nine, eight* . . . then a firm hand pushes her toward the edge of the boat. One of Dr. Hall's henchmen is readying them for the plunge into the cold water. Dr. Hall steps in front of them. "The depth here is close to one hundred feet. With your little meter, we should be able to locate and retrieve the artifact in short order. Keep close together." She pulls her mask on and presses the button on a large light she has in her right hand.

Brett can hear the clicks all around her as the men turn on their lights. Brett and Dr. Brown weren't given any of the spotlights. She figured this was to keep them from trying to escape. Dr. Hall puts her hand up in the air with five fingers up. She lowers one finger, indicating the final countdown. Brett fumbles for the respirator and places it in her mouth. She begins taking slow breaths in and out. Dr. Hall drops into the water.

Brett stumbles over the edge and hits the water. The brown liquid splashes on the lens of her mask and flows slowly away, leaving small bits of sediment behind. There is a splash and Dr. Brown swims next to her. Four other splashes follow from the men accompanying them. The sound of the electrometer blips and beeps under the water—the only sound Brett can hear. Her breathing speeds up rapidly, in and out, as she bobs up and down in the water. She needs to control herself or she will be out of air before she ever makes it back to the surface.

Seven, six, five, four. Her heartbeat returns to its normal pace, and her breathing follows. *Slow. Breathe in. Breathe out.* Brett's mind is clear now. She is focused on the beeping sound of the meter. This is the most important thing at the moment. She gives Dr. Brown a shaky thumbs-up. Dr. Hall motions for them to dive, and without thinking, Brett propels herself forward and down into the water.

The brightness on the surface quickly turns to murky darkness as Brett angles herself downward toward the bottom of the river. The light from the large flashlights bounces off the suspended sediments floating in the river, turning the brown water a mustard yellow. Brett can see the black forms of the men as they swim behind her, and she can see Dr. Hall through the hazy water.

The flow of the river seems slower the deeper they go, and the weight on her back is much lighter. Brett listens to the beeping of the machine. The sound pulse beeps rhythmically as she descends deeper and deeper into the cloudy water. It is a peaceful sound and any other time the deep bass of the notes would relax her, but today the rhythm invigorates her. . The frequency of the beeps begins to increase rapidly as they continue. They should be forty or fifty feet below the surface now. The thought of breaking her maximum depth level doesn't cross Brett's mind as she listens. The fear that she felt before the drive has magically passed from her. She is calm, her breathing even a bit slower than normal as she listens to the rhythm of the electrometer. *Beep. Beep, beep. Beep, beep, beep.*

Brett can feel the pressure in her head building as they go deeper and deeper into the water. It is much colder now. A chill passes through her body as she continues downward. Dr. Hall motions just as a vast brown plain appears out of the murkiness of the river. They are at the bottom. Just as Brett's knees hit the riverbed, clouds of sediment billow up around her. "I don't need to do that," Brett says to herself as she holds out the electroscope. *Beep, beep, beep, beep.* The pattern is constant. They must be very close.

Brett floats above the floor of the river and watches for the appearance of de Soto's final resting place. She swims forward along the bottom, scanning the thick particles for any sign of a hollow log. There in front of her, about ten yards ahead, is a dark object that resembles a large log. One that would be large enough to put a full-grown man inside. Her pulse quickens as she swims forward. *Beep, beep, beep.*

Suddenly an object jets toward her from the murky bottom of the river. It is as long as her legs and as wide as her waist. Brett screams into her respirator, causing a stream of bubbles to billow out in a rush, and she loses her grip on the electroscope. It falls like a feather in a downdraft as it rides the current to the left and the right. Brett keeps her eyes on the dark object propelling toward her as she grasps the water for the beeping electronic device. Her fingers clasp around the machine as the dark object pulses and darts over her head showing a gaping mouth and whiskers. Brett's heart settles as the large channel catfish swims gracefully away into the mustard yellow depths.

Beep, beep, beep, beep. Brett searches around the sediment-filled bottom for the source of the electrical wave. It has to be around here somewhere. She is floating with her masked face inches from the floor of the river. She can see the sands and silts ripple in the slow-moving current. The flowing water is pulling her downstream, but she able to hold onto the mud to keep herself in one spot.

Dr. Hall swims beside her, holding a spotlight the size of a car tire. The yellow light radiating out from the bulb comes out in streaks, making the murky yellow water even more yellow. Brett welcomes the light as she runs her hands through the loose material, searching for the hollow log holding de Soto. If she can find the log, she will have the cross. She will need to figure out how to escape after that.

Brett checks her air gauge on a strap near her collarbone. The red needle is fluttering back and forth. She taps it with her finger and the dial settles on a thick black line in the middle of the gauge. She starts counting. *Ten, nine, eight.* She is going to have to hurry now.

She kicks her feet. The beeping never stops. They are right on top of it, but the river bottom is smooth. There isn't a log or even any fragments of logs present. She looks down at the beeping electrometer. She glances to her left and can see the wide eyes of Dr. Brown through her foggy mask. Brett glances toward Biven Hall and sees her bright eyes dancing in the yellow light. She looks deranged as she stares at the surface below Brett's hands.

It has to be here, Brett thinks. Her head begins throbbing, and she can feel the blood pulsing through her veins as the pain increases. Brett forces her fingers into the thick mud at the bottom of the river. She can no longer hear the incessant beeping from the electroscope. She spreads her fingers outward in the gooey material, searching for the cross.

The sediment is up to her elbows, and still nothing. Brett finds herself breathing faster and faster, using up the oxygen her tank much faster than she would like. If she continues with these short quick breaths there won't be much left in her tank for the trip to the surface. She forces her hands deeper into the loose river bottom frantically working her fingers through the fine grains of wet sediment. The thought of running out of air clouds her mind. She doesn't want to become a permanent fixture in the bottom of the river. She doesn't want to end up buried down here below the murky cold water.

Brett plunges deeper. Her cold fingers scrape across something smooth and metallic. She pushes the sediment away . . . and there, in the glow of Dr. Hall's cascading yellow spotlight, is a perfectly preserved golden cross. She closes her right hand around the hilt and pulls it free from the surrounding mud. She holds it up in the light. She can see Dr. Hall's eyes grow even brighter than before. Dr. Hall points to the surface. Brett nods.

Brett holds the cross to her chest, pressing it firmly against her body. She isn't going to lose this. This relic hasn't been seen in close to five hundred years. The pressure building in her head causes her eyes to water. It feels like her eyeballs are going to come sailing out of their sockets and smash into the lens of her mask. Her breaths are coming in short rasps as she tries to force oxygen into her lungs. She starts to see little red and blue lights popping in front of her eyes like a firework show. Her mind is lethargic, and she is having a difficult time remembering what she is doing. The short rapid breaths have depleted her tank.

Every breath is deeper and faster, but there isn't any oxygen left in her tank. She looks up to the surface and can see the rays of sunlight filtering through the cloudy water. She spits the mouthpiece out of her mouth and grinds her teeth together. She is going to make it. She is bringing this cross back. Brett kicks wildly upward. It feels like an eternity, but she finally breaks through the surface of the water. She spits and sputters, taking in a deep breath of hot, heavy air as she rises up and down on the current, clutching the beautiful cross to her body.

After a dozen deep breaths, Brett turns and looks around. She can see Natalie, twenty yards away, jumping up and down on the deck of the pontoon boat, waving her arms frantically. She can see the five men and Dr. Hall swimming toward the boat. Suddenly the motor fires on the pontoon boat, sending a blue plume of smoke drifting in the humid air. The boat lurches away from the lake cruiser, rocking to the left and right as it plows through the wake on the turbid water. Brett can see Natalie up on deck, rocking with the motion of the boat. She fears that Natalie might be thrown overboard, but Natalie is waving her hands wildly.

The boat plows through the waves, sending brown water flying through the air. Grandpa Jake is behind the wheel steering it with force. It races directly toward the men and Dr. Hall. The men struggle through the choppy river to the left and right of the oncoming boat. The silver pontoons seem to be growing larger and larger with each passing second. Dr. Hall is screeching over the hum of the engine. The boat is almost on top of her before she dives down under the water. Brett hears a loud *thud* as the boat passes over the top of Dr. Hall.

Brett watches as the pontoon races toward her. As it nears her, the motor slows to a soft purr. The vessel tilts forward and backward as it comes alongside her. Dr. Brown is cutting through the water beside her as she moves toward the stopped boat. Brett swims with one arm to the rear of the boat, throws her free arm onto the rigid surface, and pulls herself out of the water. She stands up on deck with the pale golden cross pressed against her chest.

Natalie rushes over to her and grips her in the strongest, rib-cracking hug she has ever received. "Thank God you're alive," Natalie says as she squeezes her tighter.

"There is less pressure at the bottom of the river," Brett says in a strained voice. "And it almost killed me."

"You're crazy, you know that?" Natalie steps back. Brett looks down at the cross and holds it up so Natalie can see it. It feels much heavier without the help of the water—at least fifteen pounds. Brett struggles to keep it lifted with her exhausted muscles.

Natalie's hand covers her open mouth as she stares at the cross. She reaches out and touches the smooth, glistening surface. "Wow! This is amazing." Brett hasn't really examined the treasure yet. She had to fight to bring the artifact up from the depths of the river. Dr. Brown stands beside her, and Brett's mind quickly returns to their current predicament. She runs over to the metallic railing and searches the muddy water for the men or Dr. Hall.

The men are moving through the water with the speed of Olympic swimmers as they near the lake cruiser. Brett scans the surface for Dr. Hall, but she can't see her. "We have to go, now!" she yells.

"Aye, aye," Grandpa Jake says smiling from behind the controls. He pushes the throttle forward, and the pontoon boat lifts out of the water and skims along the surface as it picks up speed. Brett watches as the cruiser gets further and further from them. Brett can feel the shakiness in her overused leg muscles. They feel heavy and lethargic. They are ready to stop working. She stumbles over to the bench under the green canopy and falls onto the cushion. She leans her head back and watches the billowing white clouds migrating slowly across the sky.

She takes a deep breath. She has found it. She found the cross. Now she just wants to rest. She can focus on finding Gausili tomorrow. Right now, she just wants to close her eyes and relax like a normal eleven-year-old girl. As her mind ventures toward the blackness of rest, Natalie flops down on the bench next to her, jostling her awake. "Did you see him?" she asks in a whisper. "Did you see de Soto?" Brett slowly opens her eyes. The realization that de Soto wasn't there causes her to think deeply. He died in 1542 and was placed in a hollow log and thrown into the river. "It has been four hundred and seventy-eight years," she says stoically. "The catfish and the current probably broke the log and scattered his remains all over the bed of the river."

"He wasn't there?" Natalie asks.

"Just this," Brett says, holding up the heavy cross.

Natalie stares at the simple golden symbol. "Can I hold it?" she asks with her hand outstretched.

"Of course," Brett replies, handing her the cross. As Brett places the cross in her outstretched hands, Natalie's arms sink toward the floor from the weight of the gold.

"This is heavy." Brett nods.

"How did you guys escape?" Brett says with her head tilted to the side. Natalie looks up from the cross and a smile stretches across her face. She pulls the cross back and holds it like it is a baseball bat. "Softball champ," she says, mimicking a baseball swing. "Grandpa Jake pretended he was having a heart attack, and when they went to check on him, I picked up the wooden pole they use to rescue people and I knocked them out cold." She sticks her tongue out and flutters her eyes. "Then we jumped on this and came and got you two."

Brett smiles as she listens to the story. She looks at Grandpa Jake as he steers the vessel along the east side of the river. His eyes are focused on the path ahead and he doesn't see her watching him. Brett looks behind them and waits for the large cruiser to race up the river after them. After a few minutes of watching, she is satisfied that they have escaped from the trackers.

Dr. Brown sits down next to Brett. "Where to now?" she asks, eyeing the cross in Natalie's hand. Brett runs her fingers through her damp blonde hair and looks up at Dr. Brown. She holds the cross up.

"We go away from the setting sun to Gausili," Brett says as she stares out at the wide river flowing south and remembers the words of Ortiz. Those were words she could not forget.

CHAPTER 13

Found in the Moonlight

The trip from Greenville, Mississippi back to the mountains of east Tennessee seems to take forever. The six hundred miles took twelve hours to trek, and Brett finds it difficult to sleep. She has her field book out on her lap, the cross placed securely in the fold between the pages. A headlamp she wears illuminates the cross and the pages of her book. She is studying the pages with the flawless, looping handwriting about Ortiz. If he found Gausili in eastern Tennesse, why did de Soto take the cross west? She has been searching for the answer to that question since they drove through Knoxville.

She looks out at the night sky gliding by the Ford Escape. The purple hues and blinking stars overhead are quite peaceful, and she can feel the tension in her body starting to release. She runs her hand along the main stem of the faded golden cross. She can feel a slight tingle in the tips of her fingers as she grazes the smooth, metallic surface. There is a rhythm to the pulses, *beep, beep, beep— beep, beep, beep, beep, beep.* Brett keeps her fingers on the conductive metal. There is a pause in the signal, but a second later it continues: *beep, beep, beep, beep, beep, beep, beep, beep—beep, beep.*

She closes her eyes, feeling the same cadence of impulses flowing from the cross into her waiting finger. The first rhythm begins repeating: *beep, beep, beep....* There is a pause, then the second set starts again.

Brett's eyes flutter as she focuses her mind on what this could be. What is the cross trying to tell her? De Soto believed the cross could locate other locations of importance. The Nunnehi told her that the object could help her find her father. The cross is a meter for locating anomalies. The seven golden cities are creating anomalies in our space and time.

As the pulsing continues, Brett begins to notice a distinctive number pattern that is almost musical. When she took bass guitar lessons, the teacher always told her to feel the rhythm. She would move her index and middle finger in counts of four. One, two, three, four, with varying speeds depending on the speed of the note.

Brett's eyes dart open. "They are numbers," she says softly. "They are numbers! Three . . . five . . . eight . . . two," she says louder. Natalie jumps beside her and begins looking out the back of the car.

"Did they find us?" she stammers.

"What do they mean?" Brett asks, leaning her head back against the seat.

"You nearly gave me a heart attack," Natalie says, closing her eyes. "Wake me up first the next time you decide to scream."

Brett writes "three, five – eight, two" in her field book. She runs her fingers through her hair, trying to force her mind into action.

"Dr. Brown?" Brett asks. "What do you think these numbers mean?"

"I'm not sure. But it sounds like they are in a sequence."

"The cross is repeating the numbers."

Natalie sits up and looks down at the pages of the book. "Repeating the numbers?" She looks at Brett as if she has lost her mind. Brett grabs her hand and quickly places it on the pulsing metal of the cross. "Oh my," Natalie stammers. "I can feel it going into my fingers." Natalie looks down at the book again.

Brett shakes her head. "I thought they might have been times, but the numbers don't fit."

Grandpa Jake turns around. "Back when I was in the army, we used numbers like that to indicate locations."

Brett stops breathing for a few seconds. A location. Could it be a location? Thirty-five and eighty-two. "Those are longitude and latitude measures," Brett exclaims, hitting herself on the head with the palm of her hand. "Grandpa, that is awesome."

Grandpa Jake smiles. "Finally contributed."

"Exactly," Brett laughs. "We wouldn't be here without you."

Natalie thrusts her phone in front of Brett's face. "Thirty-five degrees by eighty-two degrees is close to the spot where we visited those protectors of the mountain. I would say five miles from that point at the top of the mountain."

"De Soto found Gausili, and he used this to find the other cities," Brett says confidently.

"What are you talking about now?"

"Why did we find it in the Mississippi River?" Brett says. "He was using it to locate the other cities. If this thing gives the exact locations, he would know exactly where they were hidden."

"You think that is plausible?" Dr. Brown interjects.

"We found Cibola using magnetics," Brett says staring at her. "What if this can locate the exact position?"

"Then that would be extraordinary."

"That's why the goon squad came after us," Natalie says.

Brett slides her fingers across the electrified golden metal. The thought that those men might try to take the cross from them worries her. "We need to find Gausili before they get there," Brett says, glancing over at Natalie. Natalie nods her head.

"Mom, we need to head east out of Newport toward the French Broad River." Brett is the closest she has been to finding her dad in months, and this time she doesn't plan on failing.

* * * * *

They drive through the early morning darkness around bends and sharp curves on the two-lane street. The moon illuminates the road ahead as Dr. Brown turns right off the main highway and travels up a slightly elevated grade along a gravel road. The rocks beat on the metal of the frame as the tires kick the rocks upward. "We are almost there," Natalie says staring at her phone.

Dr. Brown slows down. "Looks like we are out of road," she says, hitting the brakes and stopping the car.

"I guess we walk from here," Brett says as she looks out into the moonlit morning. The deep purple night is starting to grow paler as the first streaks of light filter over the mountains.

"That was in Indiana Jones, wasn't it?" Natalie laughs. A half-smile forms on Brett's face.

"Thought it was fitting."

Brett takes the cross from her book and holds it in her right hand. She takes her field book and shoves it into her bag. "Time to shine." She throws open the door and steps out into the cool morning air, taking a deep breath as she throws her backpack over her shoulder.

She can smell the fresh pine and cedar as she walks toward the dark tree line. The cross is vibrating in her hand as she continues. The current flowing into her hand and fingers pulses faster as she approaches the looming forest. Natalie runs up beside her with her phone outstretched. The screen lights up her face. "Should be another hundred yards or so up that slope. Along the dark and creepy path," she says as she examines the bright screen and then looks up at the trail through the swaying trees.

Brett pushes through a long-needle pine branch protruding out into the pathway. Ten feet further and Brett almost drops the cross onto the leaf-strewn ground as the electrical pulse sends bolts of pain through her flesh and down into the bones of her hand. Her spasming fingers and the tremors rolling through her body catch Natalie's attention. "Is the cross causing that?" she asks, concerned. "Maybe you should put it in your bag." Brett shakes her head defiantly. She isn't going to let it out of her sight. She is so close to something, she can deal with a little discomfort.

Brett and Natalie walk side by side up the narrow pathway. The slope becomes steep and rocky as gravity has forced the boulders from the top to reposition themselves along the edges of the incline. Brett looks behind her as she stops to catch her breath. She can see the movements of Dr. Brown and Grandpa Jake below them. "Grandpa Jake?" Brett yells. "How are you doing back there?"

"Just fine," Grandpa Jake says in a strained voice. They are only ten yards behind them, and as they move through the thicket Brett can see them fully. She jumps down from the tall rock.

"We are almost there, Grandpa." Natalie walks a few paces in front of Brett, using the light from her cell phone to show the path.

"It looks like it is flattening out up ahead," Natalie says confidently. The excitement builds inside Brett and her pace quickens. She jumps over the logs and boulders that litter the path. The adrenaline coursing through her body masks the painful electrical current flowing into her from the cross.

A light humming sound slowly fills the air as Natalie and Brett continue upward. "Do you hear that?" Natalie asks. It resembles the low rumble of an electrical transformer that has just been turned on. The noise pulses in the air from low frequency to high frequency.

"We must be close," Brett says

Suddenly small orbs of light appear out of the darkness directly in front of them. The air catches in Brett's throat as she stares at the dancing balls that oscillate from dull to bright. Her fingers are numb as she moves forward out onto the flat top of the ridge. Natalie walks beside her, so close that Brett can feel the heat coming from her arms.

"This is amazing," Brett says as she follows the shimmering lights.

"I don't think we should go any further," Natalie says with a raspy voice, but Brett isn't going to stop. This is the route to her father, and she is almost there. Natalie's cell phone screen instantly flashes brightly, and as they step forward the electrical signal flowing into Brett's hand stops. Brett looks down at the cross. It appears to be glowing.

"Oh," Natalie says as she sees the radiating light. "This is getting weird. Maybe we should wait for mom and Grandpa Jake." Brett shakes her head.

"We have to find Gausili." Brett looks at Natalie with an expression that says, "This is the only way." Natalie wrinkles her nose and nods in agreement.

The girls step forward together into the midst of the pulsing, floating orbs. Natalie holds her hands over her ears as the high pitch of the electrical discharge fills the air. Instantly a bright, blinding light flashes before them as the humming sound pulses and stops. Brett and Natalie try shielding their eyes, but the light is still blinding. Red and blue spots pop into the air as Brett tries to blink away the brightness. As the light fades, Brett regains her sight—and finds herself staring at a tall stone wall with gold dust sprinkled on the edges.

"Where are we?" Natalie says breathlessly.

"Gausili?" Brett responds with her mouth agape.

Brett stares up in amazement at the towering structure. The walls have to be at least twelve feet tall, and a few feet thick. As she studies the walls of the beautiful golden city, Natalie taps her on the shoulder repeatedly. "What is it?" Brett says impatiently. She looks at Natalie and sees that she is pale and swaying from right to left. Natalie points down the pathway toward their starting point. Brett's eyes get wide as she sees a flat, grassy plain situated beside a slow-moving, pearly blue stream.

"Where did the mountain go?" Natalie asks, almost in tears. "Where are mom and Grandpa Jake?"

Brett shakes her head slowly. She isn't sure where they are, but they are no longer on the ridge outside Newport, Tennessee. They have been transported to some other place. "This isn't good," Natalie says through tears.

"No . . . it isn't," Brett says as she turns from the slow-moving river and looks up at the golden walls.

The End

About the Author

John V. Suter is an author and teacher that enjoys a good treasure hunt. He lives on a farm in Sale Creek, Tennessee with his wife and two children.

References

Andrews, Daniel Marshall, "De Soto's Route from Cofitachequi in Georgia to Cosa in Alabama," *American Anthropologist*, https://anthrosour ce.onlinelibrary.wiley.com/doi/pdf/10.1525 /aa.1917.19.1.02a00090

"Cherokee Legends," Native Languages, http:// www.native-languages.org/cherokee-legends .htm

"Hernando de Soto," Georgia Historical Society, https://georgiahistory.com/education-outre ach/online-exhibits/featured-historical-figur es/hernando-de-soto/death-and-legacy/